FLIGHT OF A WITCH

ALSO BY ELLIS PETERS

FLIGHT OF A WITCH

ELLIS PETERS

THE MYSTERIOUS PRESS
New York · Tokyo · Sweden · Milan
Published by Warner Books

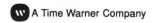 A Time Warner Company

3304

First published in Great Britain by William Collins
Copyright © 1964 by Ellis Peters
All rights reserved.

Mysterious Press books are published by
Warner Books, Inc., 666 Fifth Avenue, New York, NY 10103.
Ⓦ A Time Warner Company

The Mysterious Press name and logo are
trademarks of Warner Books, Inc.

Printed in the United States of America
First U.S. printing: May 1991

10 9 8 7 6 5 4 3 2 1

Library of Congress Cataloging-in-Publication Data

Peters, Ellis, 1913–
    Flight of a witch / Ellis Peters.
        p.   cm.
    "Previously published in England by Collins"—T.p.verso.
    ISBN 0-89296-404-9
    I. Title.
PR6031.A49F5   1991
823'.912—dc20   90-84895
                                                           CIP

Book design by Giorgetta Bell McRee

FLIGHT OF A
WITCH

CHAPTER 1

Driving along the lane from Fairford, at four o'clock on that half-term Thursday in October, Tom Kenyon saw Annet Beck climb the Hallowmount and vanish over the crest.

A shaft of lurid light sheared suddenly through the rain clouds to westward and lit upon the rolling, dun-colored side of the hill, rekindling the last brightness in the October grass. The rift widened, spilling angry radiance down the slope, and a moving sapphire blazed into life and climbed slowly upward through the bleached and faded green. The blue of her coat had seemed dark and unobtrusive when she had stood at the gate, holding him off with eyes impenetrable as stone; it burned now with the deep fire of the brightest of gentians.

And what was she doing there, in the cleft of brightness between rain and rain, like an apparition, like a portent?

He pulled in to the curve of rutted grass in front of the Wastfield gate and stopped the car there. He watched her mount, and nursed the small spark of grievance against her jealously, because for some reason it seemed to him suddenly threatened by some vast and obliterating dark that rendered it precious and comforting by contrast.

Westward, the folded hills of Wales receded into leaden cloud, but on the near side of the border the Hallowmount flaunted its single ring of ancient, decrepit trees in an orange-red like the reflected glow of fire. The speck of gentian-blue climbed to the crest, stood erect against the sky for an instant, shrank, vanished. And at the same moment the rent in the clouds closed and sealed again, and the light went out.

The hill was dark, the circle of soft October rain unbroken. He turned the ignition key, and let the Mini roll back over the glistening, pale grass onto the road. Maybe three hours of daylight left, if this could be called daylight, and with luck he could be home in Hampstead soon after dark. His mother would have a special supper waiting for him, his father would probably go so far as to skip his usual Thursday evening bridge in his son's honor, and more than likely Sybil would drop round with careful casualness about nine o'clock, armed with some borrowed magazines to return, or some knitting patterns for his mother; having, of course, a matter of weeks ago, taken care to inform herself as to when Comerbourne Grammar School kept its half-term, and whether he was coming down by car or by train. She would want to hear all about his new school, about his sixth form and their academic records, and his digs, and all the people he had met, and all the friends he had made, to the point of exhaustion. But if he told her any of the essentials she would be completely lost.

How do you interpret a semifeudal county on the Welsh borders to a daughter of suburbia? Especially when you are yourself a son of suburbia, a townie born and bred, quick but inaccurate of perception, brash, uncertain among these immovable families and seats of primeval habitation, distracted between the sophistication of these elegant border women, active and emancipated, and those dark racial memories of theirs, that mold so much of what they do and say? Sybil had no terms of reference. She would be as irrelevant and lost here as he had been, that first week of term.

Mathematics, thank God, is much the same everywhere and he was a perfectly competent teacher; he had only to cling firmly to his work for a few weeks and the rest fell readily into place. He knew he could teach, headmasters didn't have to tell him that. And all things considered, the first half of his first term hadn't gone badly at all.

The school buildings were old but good, encrusted with new blocks behind, and a shade cramped for parking space, though with a Mini he didn't have to worry overmuch about that. He hadn't been prepared to find so many sons of wealthy commuting businessmen from the Black Country at school here in the marches, and their lavish standard of living had somewhat daunted him, until he ran his nose unexpectedly into the headmaster's characteristic notice on the hall board:

"Will the Sixth Form please refrain from encroaching on the Staff parking ground, as their Jaguars and Bentleys are giving the resident 1955 Fords an inferiority complex."

That had set him up again in his own esteem. And the long-legged seventeen- and eighteen-year-olds who emerged from the parental cars, in spite of their resplendent transport, were not otherwise hopelessly spoiled, and had a shrewd grasp of the amount of work that would keep them out of trouble, and an equable disposition to produce the requisite effort, with a little over for luck. They seemed to Tom Kenyon at once more mature and developed and more spontaneous and young than the southern product with which he was more familiar, and on occasions, when they were shaken out of their equilibrium by something totally unexpected, alarmingly candid and abrupt. But they were resilient; they recovered their balance with admirable aplomb. Usually they were pulling his leg before he'd realized they no longer needed nursing. They weren't a bad lot.

Even the staff were easy enough. Even the three women for whom he hadn't been prepared. Jane Darrill, the junior geographer, could be a bit offhand and you-be-damned when she liked, but of course she was very young, not above twenty-five. Tom was twenty-six himself.

It was Jane who had suggested he should move out to the village of Comerford for living quarters, and put him in touch with the Becks, who had a house too big for them, and an income, on the whole, rather too small.

"If you're going to be a countryman," said Jane, with her suspiciously private smile that always made his hackles rise a little in the conviction that she was somehow making fun of him, "you might as well go the whole hog and be a proper one. Come and be a borderer, like me. Comerford is the real thing. This dump is rapidly becoming a suburb of Birmingham."

That was an exaggeration, or perhaps a prophecy.
Jane was blessed, or cursed, with an appearance of
extreme competence and cheerfulness, round-faced,
fair-complexioned, vigorous, pretty enough if she
hadn't filed her brusque manner to an aggressive
edge in order to keep the Lower Sixth in healthy awe
of her. Sometimes she liked to offset the impression
by leaning perversely toward cynicism and gloom.

Tom looked out of the common-room window upon
a Comerbourne which appeared to his urban eye
small, limited, antique and charming. He could see
the tops of the limes in the riverside gardens, a thin
ribbon of silver, the balustrade of the nearer bridge
over the Comer. A provincial capital of the minor
persuasion, still clinging to its weekly country mar-
ket, still drawing in, to buy and sell, half the house-
wives and farmwives of a quarter of Wales as well as
Midshire itself. Back streets straight out of the
Middle Ages, a few superb Tudor pubs, a dwindling
county society more blood-ridden and exclusive
than he'd thought possible in the midtwentieth century, still conscientiously freezing out intruders,
and pathetically unaware that its island of privilege
had long since become an island of stagnation in a
backwater of impotence, and was crumbling away
piecemeal from under its large, sensibly shod feet;
and round it and over it, oblivious of it, swarmed the
busy, brisk, self-confident rush of the new people,
the new powers, business and banking and industry
and administration, advancing upon an expanding
future, brushing with faint impatience and no ceremony past the petrified remnants of a feudal past.

That was what he saw in Comerbourne; and to tell
the truth, the encroachments of the industrial Mid-
lands into the fossilized life of this remote capital
rather attracted than repelled him. But he'd never

lived in a village, and the idea still had a (probably quite misleading) charm about it. He thought vaguely of country pursuits and country functions, and saw himself adopted into a village society which would surely not be averse to finding a place for a young and presentable male, whatever his origins. He could have the best of both worlds, with Comerbourne only a couple of miles away, near enough to be reached easily when he needed it, far enough away to be easily evaded when he had no need of it. And it's always a good idea to put at least a couple of miles between yourself and your work in the evenings.

"What are these Becks like?" he asked, half in love with the idea but cautious still.

"Oh, ordinary. Middle-aged, retired, a bit stodgy, maybe. Terribly conscientious; they'll probably worry about whether they're doing enough for you. Not amusing, but then you needn't rely on them for your amusement, need you? Mr. Beck used to teach at the Modern until a couple of years ago. He never made it to a headship. Not headmaster material," she said rather dryly. Tom Kenyon, confident, clever, and ambitious, was obvious headmaster material, and, moreover, knew it very well.

"He hasn't got a son here, has he?" asked Tom sharply, suddenly shaken by the thought of having his landlady's darling under his feet, with a fond mamma pushing persuasively behind. He wished it back the moment it was out. A silly question. Jane wouldn't be such a fool as to land him in any such situation; it would be against all her teacher's instincts, and they were shrewd and effective enough. And blurting out the horrid thought had only exposed himself. But she merely gave him the edge of a deflationary smile, and rattled away half a dozen rock specimens into the back of her table drawer.

"No sons at all, don't worry. 'He has but one daughter, an uncommon handsome gel.'"

"Go on!" He wasn't particularly interested, but he produced the spark in the eye and the sharpening glow of attention that was demanded of him, and straightened his tie with exaggeratedly fatuous care. "How old?"

"Eighteen. I think! She was seventeen last spring, anyhow, when the row—" She frowned and swallowed the word, shoving away papers; but he hadn't been listening closely enough to demand or even miss the rest of the sentence.

"Eighteen, and uncommon handsome! That does it! They won't look at me, they'll be after some old gorgon of a maiden aunt for a lodger."

Jane turned her fashionable shock-head of mangled brown hair and grinned at him derisively. "Come off it!" she said. "You're not that dangerous." It had been a joke, and all that, but she needn't have sounded so crushingly sure of herself. Girls had never given him much trouble, except by clinging too long and tightly, and at the wrong times.

"What's her name?" he asked.

"Annet."

"Not Annette?"

"Not Annette. Just Annet. Plain Annet."

"What's plain about it? Annet Beck. That's a witch's name."

"Annet is a witch, I shouldn't wonder." Jane looked thoughtfully back into the past again, and refrained from calling attention to what she saw. Witch or not, neither of them was greatly concerned with Annet; not then. "Go and take a look at the place, anyhow," said Jane, offhand as usual. "If you don't like the look of the border solitude, you needn't take it any further."

And he had gone, and he had taken the recommended look at Comerford. Along the riverside road, through coppices scarlet and gold with autumn, and thinning to filigree; out of sight and memory of the town, between farms rising gently from water meadows to stubble to heath pasture, over undulations of open ground purple with heather, and down to the river again.

The village closed in its ford from either bank, a compact huddle of old houses, considerably larger than he had expected, and comparatively sophisticated, with beautiful converted cottages and elegant gardens on its fringes that told plainly of pioneering commuters or wealthy retired business people in possession. The town had, in fact, reached Comerford; it was almost a small town itself. He looked at it, and was disappointed. But when he lifted his eyes to look over it, and saw the surging animal backs of the enfolding hills, time ran backwards over his head like silk unwinding from a dropped spool.

Ridge beyond ridge, receding into pallor and mist, filmed over with the oblique beams of light splayed from behind broken copper cloud, Wales withdrew into fine rain, while England lay in quivering, cool sunlight. Meadows and dark, low hedges climbed the slopes. Away on the dwindling flank of the hogback to northwestward the horizontal scoring of ancient mine levels showed plainly. Lead, probably, worked out long since, or at any rate long since abandoned. Round the crest of the same hill the unquestionable green earthworks of an Iron Age fort, crisp and new-looking as though it had been molded only yesterday. The long green heavings of turf, the deep ditches, the few broken, black mine

chimneys and the gunmetal-colored heaps of old
spoil nested together without conflict, and the village with its smart new facades and its congealing
shopping streets settled comfortably in the lee of the
scratched Roman workings, and thought no wrong.
All time was relative here; or perhaps all time was
contemporaneous. Nothing that was native was
alien or uncanny here, though it came from the
predawn twilight before man stood upright and
walked.

He drove through Comerford, village or town,
whatever it was, and the hills melted and reassem-
bled constantly as he drove, drawn back like filmy
green curtains to uncover further recessions of crest
beyond crest. Arthur Beck's house was beyond,
shaken loose from the last handhold of the village
itself, a quarter of a mile along a narrow but metaled
road that served a succession of border farms. On
his right the river narrowed to a trickle of trout
stream in its flat meadows along the valley floor,
winding bewilderingly, the hills grown brown and
fawn with bleached grass and sedge and coarse
heather behind. On his left a long, bare ridge of hill
crowded the road implacably nearer and nearer to
Wales. A ring of gnarled, half-naked trees, by their
common age and their regular arrangement clearly
planted by man, showed like a topknot on the crest.
One outcrop of rock broke the blond turf halfway up,
another had shown for a few moments over the comb
of the ridge, a little apart from the trees on the
summit. Sheep paths, trampled out daintily over
centuries by ancestors of these handsome, fearless
hill sheep he was just learning to know for Cluns and
Kerrys, traced necklets round the slopes, level
above level like the courses of a step pyramid.

For the first time he was driving by the Hallowmount. The midafternoon sun was on the entire barren, rustling, pale brown slope of it, and yet he felt something of shadow and age and silence like a coolness cutting him off from the sun, not unpleasantly, not threateningly, rather as if he was naturally excluded from what embraced all other creatures here. He was the alien, not resented, not menaced, simply not belonging. And suddenly he was aware of the quietness and the permanence of this utter solitude, which seemed unpopulated, and yet had surely been inhabited ever since men began to tame beasts, before the final experimental grass seeds were ever deliberately sown, before the first stone scratched the earth, and the developing tools were smoothed to a rich polish in the manipulating hands of the first artisans.

A turn to the right, just before the track plunged into half-grown plantations of conifers, brought him down toward the river again, past the gate of Wastfield farm, through a small coppice to Arthur Beck's gate at the end of the farm wall.

There it was: Fairford. An old house, or rather a new house made from two old stone cottages, mellow, amber-colored stone from higher up the valley. A walled garden in the inevitable autumn chaos, a glimpse of rather ragged lawn, a tangle of trees too big for a garden, but beautiful. Why should he care that the leaves would be a nuisance, tread into a decaying mush all over the paths, and silt down into a rotten cement in the guttering? He wouldn't have to maintain the place; all he would have to do would be live in it and enjoy it. He imagined the summer here, and he was enchanted. Even the name wasn't an affectation, there was a fair ford only fifty yards on, where the river poured in a smooth silvery sheet above clear beds of amber and agate pebbles, bright as jewels in the sun. The masonry of the original cottages looked—how old?—three centuries at least. The place had probably been Fairford ever since the advance guard of the Danes clawed a toehold on the Welsh bank of the river here, only to be rolled back fifty miles into England, and never thrust so far again.

He was almost sure then that he would come and lodge here; but some instinct of caution and perversity turned him back from opening the gate then and advancing to the massy door. He parked the car by the open grass along the riverside instead, and went for a long walk up the flank of the hill until it was time to drive back into Comerbourne.

"Not bad," he said to Jane, in the common room during the next free period they shared, "but I don't know. All right in the summer, but a bit back-of-beyond for a bad winter, I should say. You could get snowed up there for weeks."

"They ought to charge you extra for that as an amenity," said Jane, bitterly contemplating some gem in the homework of Four B, who were not her brightest form. "Imagine having a cast-iron alibi for contracting out of this madhouse for weeks at a time! But don't kid yourself, my boy. They kept that road open even in 1947. The Wastfield tractors see to that. Snow or no snow, nobody gets away with anything around here."

She didn't ask him what he thought of doing, or he might, even then, have gone off in the opposite direction, sure that everybody has an angle, and she couldn't be totally disinterested. She lived in Comerford herself, he knew that, and hadn't failed to allow for one obvious possibility. But she showed no personal interest in him; and even if she was biding her time she wouldn't find him easy to keep tabs on, with her family's cottage a quarter of a mile this side the village, and Fairford well out on the opposite side. He'd had plenty of practice in evading girls he didn't want to see, as well as in cornering those he did. No, he needn't worry about Jane.

So he went back to Fairford on the Saturday afternoon. The westering sun smiled on him all the way along that journey back into prehistory, confirming his will to stay. By the time he drove back the dusk had closed on the Hallowmount, and black clouds covered the hills of Wales; a chill wind drove up the valley, crying in the new plantation. And he might have changed his mind, even then, if he hadn't been already lost from the moment when he rattled the knocker at Fairford, and listened to the rapid, light footsteps within as someone came to open the door to him.

He was lost, then and forever; because it was Annet who opened the door.

There is a kind of beauty that produces wolf whistles, and another kind of beauty that creates silence all about it, taking the voices out of men's mouths and the breath out of their throats. Nobody but Annet had ever struck Tom Kenyon dumb. He lived in the same house with her, he'd been rubbing shoulders with her now almost daily for half a term, and still he went softly for awe of her, and the words that would have come to him so glibly with a girl who meant nothing to him ebbed away clean out of mind when he was face to face with this girl. And yet why? She was flesh and blood like anyone else. Wasn't she?

(But why, why should she be climbing the Hallowmount in the rain and the murk in a dank October twilight? Distant and strange and elusive as she was, what could draw her up there at such an hour of such a day?)

She was not much above middle height for her eighteen years, but so slender that she looked tall, and taller still because of the lofty way she carried her small head, tilted a little back to let the great, soft masses of her hair fall back from her face. When she wanted to hide she sat with head bent, and the twin black curtains, blue-black, burnished, smooth and heavy, drew protective shadows over her face. She wore it cut in a long bob, not quite to her shoulders, uncurled, uncolored, unfashionable, parted over her left temple, the ends curving under to touch her neck. He never saw her play with it; the most she ever did was lift a hand to thrust it back out of her way; and yet every gleaming hair clung to the sheaf as threads of silk cling, alive and vital, and even after streaming in the wind the heavy coils flowed back massively like water into their constant order and repose.

Between the wings of this resplendent helmet her face was oval, delicate and still, with fine bones that impressed their pure, taut shapes through the creamy flesh. Passionate, eloquent bones, if the envelope that enclosed them had not imposed its own ivory silence upon them. There was little red in her face, and yet she was not pale; when he saw her first she had the gloss of the summer still upon her, and was tinted with honey. Her mouth was grave and full, often sullen, often sad, quick to smile, but never at any joke he could share, or any pleasure he could afford her. And her eyes were the deep, brilliant, burning blue the sun had just found in her coat on the crest of the Hallowmount, the blue of the darkest gentians, between blue-black lashes as dark as her hair.

She had showed him the room, and he had taken

the room, hardly aware of its pleasant furnishings,
seeing only the movement of her hand as she opened
the door, and the long, courteous, unsmiling blue
stare that had never wavered as she waited for him
to speak. Her own voice was deep and quiet, and
only now did he realize how few words he had ever
heard it speak, to him or to anyone. She moved like
a true eighteen-year-old, with a rapid, coltish grace.
What she did about the house was done well and
ungrudgingly, but with a certain impatience and a
certain resignation, as though she were making
ritual gestures which she knew to be indispensable,
but in the efficacy of which she did not believe. And
her attendance on him was of the same kind; it hurt
and bewildered him to know it, but he could not
choose but know.

For him life in Fairford had only gradually taken
shape as a frame for Annet, and all the kaleidoscope
of other faces that peopled his new world was only a
galaxy in attendance upon her. Arthur Beck, handsome in a feeble, pedantic way, wisps of thin hair
carefully arranged over his high crown, glasses
askew on his precipitous nose, bore about with him
always an air of vague and puzzled disappointment,
and a precarious and occasionally pompous dignity.
Aging people shouldn't have children, when they
were doomed to be always so hopelessly far from
them. Even the mother must have been nearly forty
at the time. Who can jump clean over forty years?

Mrs. Beck, solider and more decisive than her
husband, was one of the plainest women Tom had
ever seen, and yet revealed a startling echo of
Annet's beauty sometimes in a look or a movement.
Dark hair without luster, waved crisply and immov-
ably, dark blue eyes faded into a dull, grayish color,
like blue denim after a lifetime of washing, an

anxious face, kind but troubled, a flat, practical voice.

Dull, impenetrable people, at least to a newcomer with more self-assurance than patience. And that incredible bud of their age flowered with face turned away from them, as though her sun had always risen elsewhere.

The children of aging marriages, so he had heard, are often difficult and strange, like deprived children; in a sense they are deprived, a lost generation cuts them off from their roots, they have grandparents for parents. These were not even young grandparents at heart, but dim, discouraged and old. Sometimes gleams of wistful scholarship showed in Beck, and brought a momentary eagerness back to his face. Mrs. Beck kept up with village society, and dressed like a county gentlewoman, but for God's sake, what good was that when county gentlewomen were themselves a generation out of date, living anachronisms, museum pieces even here, where the past, the genuine past, was as real and valid as tomorrow?

At first he had thought, with his usual healthy confidence in his own charms, that he would bring a breath of fresh air into Annet's enclosed life, and provide her with the young company she needed. But in a week or two he had found that she was, in fact, almost never in, and appeared to have gallingly little need of him. She had a job that took her away during the day; she acted as secretary to Mrs. Blacklock at Cwm Hall, a privilege which gave great satisfaction to her mother, if she herself accepted it without noticeable emotion. The lady needed a secretary, for she ran, it seemed to Tom, everything in sight, every local society, every committee, every charity, every social event. Nothing could take place

in and around Comerford without Regina's blessing.
Her patronage of Annet, therefore, was balm to Mrs.
Beck's heart. Annet, as Tom heard from various
sources—but never from Annet!—would have liked
to uproot herself from this backwater and go and get
a job in London, but the Becks were terrified to let
her, and had stubbornly refused to consent. Maybe
because they knew they were hopelessly out of
touch with her, and were afraid to let her out of their
sight; maybe because she was their ewe lamb, and
they couldn't bear to part with her. She was safe
with Mrs. Blacklock. Regina was inordinately careful and kind. Regina never let her come home alone
if she was at all late, but sent her in the car. Regina
wouldn't let her strike up any undesirable acquain-
tances, Regina saw to it that she knew everyone who
was presentable and of good repute.

For God's sake, thought Tom impotently, she was
eighteen, wasn't she? And intelligent and capable, or
the Blacklocks wouldn't have kept her. And did she
behave as if she needed a chaperone?

She lived a busy enough life. Choir practice on
Friday nights, dances in Comerbourne on Satur-
days, or cinemas, and Myra Gibbons from Wastfield
usually went with her. Their escorts to dances were
vetted carefully; Mrs. Beck had old-fashioned notions. But the sorry fact remained that Annet had no
need of Tom Kenyon. There wasn't a young man in
Comerford who hadn't at some time paid tentative
court to her. There wasn't a young man in Comerford
who had got further with her than he found himself
getting.

Remote, alien and beautiful, Annet floated upon
the tide of events, submitted to parental control
without comment or protest, and kept her own
secrets. He didn't know her at all; he never would.

The rest revolved about her. They had made him welcome, adopted him readily into their activities, found him a part to play; more than she ever had. Yet he saw them only by her light, at least those nearest to her: the Blacklocks, the vicar with his hearty voice and his uncertain, deprecating eyes, the Gibbons family, all the population of Fairford. Lucky for him that some of the denizens of his Sixth lived in Comerford, and their parents opened their doors to him readily: Miles Mallindine's young, modern parents, Dominic Felse's policeman father and pretty, shrewd, amusing mother. Policeman was the wrong term, strictly speaking; George Felse was a Detective-Inspector in the Midshire C.I.D., recently promoted from Detective-Sergeant. The progeny of these pleasant couples tolerated him and kept their lordly distance, behaving with princely punctilio if they were left to entertain him; the parents welcomed him and never worried him. Privately they laughed a little, affectionately, at their own sons. Tom found them a pleasure and a relief. And they delivered him, at least, from feeling himself dependent upon Annet's charity, when he had dreamed of extending to her the largesse of his own.

He drove through the dim rain, and he saw all the procession of new faces, one by one, passing before him. But always Annet, always Annet. And always with gentian eyes fixed ahead, and face turned away from him.

Eve Mallindine had given him a lift once, when the Mini was in the garage for servicing, and run him into town from the Comerford bus stop. It was pure chance that he had mentioned Annet to her; if anything connected with Annet could be called chance. More probably he was so full of her that he couldn't

keep her name out of his mouth. Had he even
betrayed that he was jealous of the young men who
danced with her at the Saturday hops in town, and
resented her mother's prim care of her? He was
horribly afraid he might have done. Well for him it
was Mrs. Mallindine. Everything a sixth-former's
mother should be, young and sophisticated and
pretty, with a twinkle in her artfully blue-shadowed
eyes, and legs like flappers used to have before the
fad for impossible shoes spoiled their gait and made
them the same thickness from ankle to knee. Inci-
dentally, she wore stiletto heels herself. How did
she manage to walk like a proud filly in them? And
how on earth did she drive so well?

She looked along her shoulder at him briefly, and
returned her golden brown eyes to the road ahead.
She pondered for a moment, and then she said, "I'd
better tell you, Tom. Do you mind if I call you Tom?
After all, you're almost *in loco parentis* to my brat."

He hadn't minded. He couldn't remember when
he'd minded anything less. Just sitting beside her
was enough to make him feel a few inches taller, and
he needed every lift he could get, when he remembered Annet.

"Barbara Beck isn't so mad as she looks to you,"
said Eve Mallindine, with a wry little smile. "Annet
nearly made a run for it, early last spring. With my
blessed hopeful. And don't you dare let him know I
told you, or I'll wring your neck. But you wouldn't,
you're not the kind. Excuse a mother's partiality. I
wouldn't like him hurt. And if I'd been seventeen and
male, I'd have jumped at the chance, too. They didn't
get any farther than Comerbourne station. Bill got
wind of it, somehow—I never asked him how, I was
far too busy pretending everything was normal and I
hadn't noticed the row going on. Bill took Annet

home, and then brought the pup back and shut himself in the bedroom with him. I'm sure they both behaved with the greatest dignity—not even a raised voice between 'em! Miles was past seventeen, and nearly six feet high, and so damned grown-up— Well, you know him! Poor Bill must have felt at a hopeless disadvantage—if he hadn't been in a flaming temper. I don't know which of them I was sorriest for. I kept out of it, and made a cheese soufflé. It seemed the most sensible thing to do, they were both crazy about my cheese soufflés, and even a brokenhearted lover has to eat." She cast a glance at him again, even more briefly, and grinned. "They argued for an hour, and neither would give an inch. Poor darlings, they're so alike. Don't you think so?"

He didn't. He saw Miles Mallindine every time he looked at her. Miles wasn't the most unattractive member of the Upper Sixth, not by a long way. But all he said was, somewhat constrainedly, "Where were they heading?"

"They had one-way tickets for London. Poor lambs, they were twenty minutes early for the train. A mistake! The trouble I had, getting Miles thawed out after that catastrophe. It's awfully difficult, you know, Tom, for a seventeen-year-old to believe one doesn't blame him. But I didn't. Would you? You've seen Annet."

"No," he said; with difficulty, but it sounded all right. "No, I wouldn't blame him."

"Good for you, Tom, I knew you were human. But poor Bill has a social conscience, you see. I only have a human one. They made each other pretty sore. Bill felt Miles ought to come right out and confide in him. And Miles wouldn't. They ate the soufflé, though," she added comfortably, rightly recollecting this as reassurance that her menfolk were

not seriously disabled, physically or emotionally.
"And to tell the truth, I laced the coffee. It seemed a
good thing to do."

Was he allowed to ask questions? And if so, how
far could he go? There must be a limit, and the most
interesting questions probably stepped well over it.
Such as: Why? Why should Miles find it necessary to
plan a runaway affair with Annet? Many escorts a
good deal less presentable were allowed to take the
girl about, provided they called for her respectably
at the house, and were vetted and found reliable.
The Becks wouldn't have frozen out a good-looking
boy with wealthy parents, excellent prospects, and
charm enough, when he pleased, to call the bird
from the tree. If he'd wanted Annet, he had only to
convince the girl; her parents would certainly have
smiled upon him from the beginning. So why? Why
run? Apparently there was no question of previous
misbehavior, no girl-in-trouble complications that
made a getaway and a quick marriage desirable.

"It's all blown over now, of course," said Eve,
slowing at the first traffic lights on the edge of
Comerbourne. "Nobody else ever treated it as more
than a romantic escapade. But Mrs. Beck still
thinks Miles planned her poor girl's ruin. I thought
I'd better tell you how the land lay, you might feel a
bit baffled if it came up out of the blue."

Somehow it was too late by then for the "why"
question. All he could say was, "And is he still—I
mean, has he got over her by now?"

"I don't know. I don't ask him. What he wants to
tell he'll tell, what he doesn't nobody can make him.
Me, I don't try. But getting over Annet might be
quite an arduous convalescence, don't you think so?"

"It well might," said Tom, with brittle care. She

was a dangerous woman; she might see all too readily that Miles wasn't the only chronic case.

"Ah, well," she said cheerfully, putting her foot down as the red changed to green, "he'll be going up to Queens' next year, and he'll have more than enough to keep him busy. I hear he's coming camping with you next weekend. Thirty juniors to ride herd on, he says. Heaven help you all!"

"We'll survive," said Tom. If you were the youngest male member of staff, and owned an anorak and a pair of clinkered boots, you were a sitter for all the outdoor assignments, and it was your bounden duty to look martyred and moan about it. No matter how much you actually enjoyed skippering a party of boys up a mountain or under canvas, you could never admit it. "Drop me along here by Cooks', would you? I've got to see about some maps I ordered."

And as he got out of the car and leaned to offer thanks for his ride, glad to be seen with her, complemented by the greetings he shared with her, the amazing woman smiled up at him confidently and calmly, and said, "You won't take them on the Hallowmount, will you?"

She wasn't even going to wait for an answer, so completely did she trust him to accept and understand what she had said. She gave him a little wave of her hand, and expected him to withdraw head and hand and close the door; and when he didn't, she sat looking up at him with a quizzical, slightly surprised smile, no doubt thinking him as endearingly male and stupid as her own pig-headed pair.

"Not take them on the Hallowmount?" said Tom cautiously, to be sure he had not mistaken her.

"No—but naturally you wouldn't. Silly of me!"

"Why not, though? Or is that a stupid question?

And why naturally not?" He had been feeling so
close to her, so comfortable with her, and suddenly
he felt alien and out of his depth. There she sat, in
her amber-and-bracken autumn suit that wouldn't
have looked abashed in Bond Street, with her
smooth brown beehive of hair and her long, elegant
legs and incredibly fragile and impractical shoes, as
modern as tomorrow, as secure and confident as
money and education and travel and native temper-
ament could make her; and without mystery or
constraint, as though she were reminding her husband to lock the garage door, she warned him off
from taking his weekend camp on the Hallowmount.

"Oh, we just wouldn't," she said, vaguely smiling,
eyes wondering at him a little, but making allowances for him, too, as the incomer, the novice in
these parts. "We just don't. I wouldn't worry too
much myself, but some of their mothers might. You
weren't thinking of going there, were you?"

"Well, no, I wasn't. Too exposed, anyhow, for
October. I was thinking of taking them up between
the Westlyns."

"Good! Fine!" said Eve Mallindine, satisfied, and
slammed the door shut. She looked up and smiled at
him through the open window. "No need to go yelling
for trouble, is there?" she said serenely, and shot
away up Castle Wylde before the lights at the Cross
could change color again.

And he had not taken them on the Hallowmount.
Once, he suspected—and the glance back at himself
when younger was revealing—he would have gone
there on principle, having been warned to keep
away. Not now. Besides, she hadn't pressed him,
hadn't exactly warned him off. She'd merely indicated to him that the plate was hot, so that he

shouldn't burn his fingers. She'd taken it for granted that no more was necessary where a sane and sensible adult was concerned. And whether it could be considered a sign of good sense and maturity or not, he hadn't taken them on the Hallowmount.

But in the gathering dark over the remnants of the fire, up there in shelter between the ridges of the Westlyns, with one ear cocked for sounds of forbidden horseplay from the Three B tents, he had turned his head to stare thoughtfully at the distant ridge of the Hallowmount, with its topknot of trees and rocks black against the milky spaces between the stars. And he had asked the son what he had never had time to ask the mother.

"How did it get its name—the Hallowmount? And why is it taken for granted one doesn't take boys camping there?"

"Is it?" said Miles vaguely, flat on his back on a spread groundsheet, with the faint glow of the fire falling aslant across his smooth, high-boned cheek and broad forehead. Mild wonder stirred in his tone and recalled Eve's look and voice, but he wasn't paying very much attention. "I suppose it would be, come to think of it. They wouldn't mind by daylight, but at night they'd probably think it wasn't the thing to do. On the principle that you never know, you know."

"I don't know," said Tom. "You tell me. What about the name, for instance?"

"I don't think anybody knows much about the name, to be honest, but a lot of them will tell you they do. It goes back into prehistory—"

"Or thereabouts," said Dominic Felse dubiously, demurring at such imprecision in his friend.

"Let's not argue about a few hundred years. Anyhow, whenever it was, we don't know how it arose.

Something not quite canny. But all this region and its inhabitants are a bit uncanny, I suppose." He opened his eyes wide at the sky and sat up, feeling it, perhaps, hardly dignified to conduct a discussion from the supine position. "Take the old lead mines," he said thoughtfully. "There couldn't be anything more practical, but there couldn't be anything more haunted, either. We have knockers—like in the Cornish tin mines. And Wild Edric's down there, too, with his fairy wife Godda. And half a dozen others, for all we know. It's the same with the Hallowmount. Some say it's 'hallow' because it was holy, a place of sacrificial mysteries in the pre-Christian cults. And some say it's really 'hollow,' and not for nothing. They say people have stumbled on the way inside sometimes, and vanished."

"Or come back years later," said Dominic helpfully, "like Kilmeny, with no memory of the time between, and as young as when they disappeared."

"Oh, that's common to every country in Europe," said Tom, disappointed. "Nearly every hill that has a striking shape or has been the site of occupation from very early times gets that tale attached to it. Are you sure King Arthur isn't down there, waiting for somebody to blow a horn and wake him up?"

"No, sir, we use Wild Edric instead round these parts, we don't need any other saviors." That was Milvers, the third of his only slightly dragooned sixth-form volunteers for this weekend chore. A clever one, Milvers, stuffed with the history and legends of the borders, all the more because he was not himself a borderer. He might be able to tell more than Miles Mallindine about the documentation of the Hallowmount; but nothing he could say would be as revealing, as perfectly direct and simple as Miles's mild, "All this region and its inhabitants are

a bit uncanny, I suppose." Without pretensions and
without reluctance he had included himself in that
verdict, in just the same way as his mother dealt
herself in. They found nothing incongruous in having
one foot in the twentieth century and one in the roots
of time.

"And some say a witch coven used to meet there,"
said Milvers, warming to the assignment. "Did you
know that outcrop of rock is known locally as the
Altar?"

He hadn't known, but it didn't surprise him. Just a
place of acquired ill omen, after all, an accumulation
of ordinary superstitions.

"So that's it," he said. "Just bad medicine."

"Oh, no, not really. Not *bad*. Any more than light-
ning's good or bad. Or fire. Or the dead." Miles
straightened and quivered to the sudden energy of
his own thoughts, the thick brown lashes rolling
back widely from bright, intent eyes. "Did somebody
tell you it was bad luck, or something?"

Tom told him, in a strictly edited version, about
that lift into town. "Your mother evidently thought it
was a place to fight shy of. I suppose that's the
legacy of the witches."

"I don't believe there ever were any witches. Just
that chain of lives going back so unbelievably far,
and a kind of impress left from them all—" He
couldn't find the words he wanted, and wouldn't
descend to substitutes; he shut his arms helplessly
around his knees, and rocked and scowled, still
mining within his mind for the means of fluency.
When not stirred, he could be a little lazy; it was an
effort getting into gear.

"Then why should everyone be afraid of it?"

Dominic looked at Miles, and Miles looked at
Dominic. Tom had seen just such exchanges pass

before, and the two mute faces relax in absolute
agreement, as now. After that it was always a
toss-up which of them would do the talking, but it
was a certainty he would be talking for both.

"We're not *afraid,*" said Miles, carefully and kindly
keeping his smile in check. "Why should we be? We
were born here. We're *in* the chain, we don't have to
be afraid of it. We belong to it."

"In awe of it, then."

They considered that with one more bright and
rapid glance, and as one man accepted it.

"Oh, in awe, yes, but that's quite another thing,
isn't it?"

"Is it so far from being afraid?" said Tom, uncon-
vinced. Miles scrambled to his knees, leaning over
the faint glow of the fire; in a little while now they
would have to smother it for the night. "When my
mother drove you into town, did she get caught at
the lights by the technical college?"

"Yes, I remember they were at red." He saw no
connection yet, but here again was the twentieth
century taking hands simply and naturally with the
primeval darkness, and he felt the continuity tightening, and his palms pricked with the foreknowl-
edge of a revelation that would leave him mute.

"And was my mother afraid?"

Patiently, willing to learn—and wasn't that something new for him too?—Tom said: "Of course not."

"No, sir, of course not. You're not afraid of traffic
lights at red, it would be silly, wouldn't it? But you
don't drive through them, either—do you?"

And he hadn't been able to pin any of them down more
precisely than that, until Jane Darrill handed him over
to the mercies of the Archaeological Society. Basely
and deliberately, as it turned out, for she must have

known very well that once they had received him as an enquirer they wouldn't let him escape until he had imbibed every word that existed in manuscript or print about the Hallowmount. They wrangled among themselves, but they spared him nothing.

Well, he'd asked for it! The vicar primed him with the parish records, and dragged him along to Miss Winslow, who kept the local archives, and Miss Winslow in turn hustled them both into the damp, dark but lovely splendors of Cwm Hall, which was middle Elizabethan black and white, and excellent of its period.

Regina Blacklock was president of the Archaeological Society as of most such bodies, and Peter Blacklock functioned as usual, good-humoredly and resignedly, as secretary and her dutiful echo. The weight of birth and position and money was all on her side; it was rather overdoing things that she should also have so strong and decisive a character. Who could stand against her? She was an authority on everything to do with Comerford and district; where the folklore of the borders was concerned, what she said went. She poured details over Tom's head in a merciless stream, buried him under evidence of the Druidic goings on that had once enlivened the Hallowmount on midsummer night and at the solstices. The vicar, pink with enthusiasm, acted as chorus whenever she drew breath. Devotees both, and no need to suspect that their passion was anything but genuine. But somehow Miles had been more convincing in his vagueness, and acceptance, and serenity.

"You must go to the Borough Library, Mr. Kenyon," said Regina, radiant with helpfulness and ardor, "you really must. I'll telephone Mr. Carling in the morning and tell him to expect you, and he'll have the Welsh chronicles ready for you whenever you'd like to call him and arrange a visit. And he has the aerial photographs of the Iron Age fort— Maeldun's Ring, you know, the one on Cleave. You should look at those, they're a revelation. Peter has a few here, but not all. Peter, darling, where are those enlargements now?"

And Peter darling brought them. Blessedly he brought a large whiskey and soda in the other hand, and a small, mild, rueful smile that warmed his long, rather tired face into a very acceptable sympathy. A tall, slender, quiet man, of spare, gentle movements and thoughtful face. Good-looking, too, in a somewhat disconsolate way, and even his mournfulness enlivened now and then by fleeting gleams of humor, affectionate when his eye dwelled upon his formidable wife, but satirical, too. They appeared to understand each other very well, but it was inevitable that she should be the one on top, since she was the last of the Wayne-Morgans, and proprietress of half this valley and one flank of the Hallowmount. Peter Blacklock had been a local solicitor by profession, though he didn't practice now, being fully employed in running his wife's estates, and making, as everyone agreed, a conscientious job of it.

How old would they be? Forty-five maybe. Not more than a year or two between them, and it could be either way. She was a very striking woman, if only she wouldn't work so hard at it; but that tremendous energy had to go somewhere, and if there were only small channels at hand to receive it they were bound to get overcharged. She expounded the history of the border as if it was the future of man. Eve Mallindine wouldn't have thought her forebears anything particular to shout about.

How well he remembered that evening. Regina

talked with passion, leaning toward him across the deep blond sheepskin rug; a big woman, red-haired but graying a little, interesting bands of silver in the short, russet hair; a broad, rather highly colored, energetic face, smooth and blond, ripe blue eyes, arched brows plucked rather too thinly; a plump, full, firm body in good country tweeds. And Peter Blacklock in his elderly, leather-elbowed sportcoat and Bedford cords, comfortable and distinguished, as though he had been born to the game. And the vicar, a contemporary, hard and athletic in body, eager and juvenile in mind, genuine echo to Mrs. Blacklock's full song. There were no pretenses here, these were the real people. Tom had never known such, and bludgeoned as he was, he could not fail to be fascinated by them.

And in the background, of course, distant, indifferent and aware, but as though her soul remained absent, Annet. Working a little late that night, as she sometimes did, bored, probably, with them all, waiting to go home. Large-eyed, motionless of face, thinking of God knew what, she watched them all and was herself so withdrawn that she might have been in another world. The heavy, soft curve of her hair shadowing her face was like the undulation of one of the cords that held the world in balance. The whiskey had been so sympathetically large that it affected his vision, and endowed her with, or perhaps only uncovered in her, cosmic significances.

"In the seventeenth century," said the vicar, glowing with ardor, "we're told there was a witch coven in these parts that used to meet on the hilltop." His voice sounded somehow lightweight and breathless, emerging from that big, lean, shapely body. I'll bet he was a Rugby blue, thought Tom inconsequently, and felt a small shock again at the uncertainty and shallowness of the face. For all his regular features, he looked more like a sixth-form schoolboy than sixth-form schoolboys themselves do nowadays. And why should he be so anxious to get in his Black Mass and his coven and his devil? But of course, he had, in a way, a vested interest in these blasphemies. Where would his profession be without them?

"Coven, nonsense!" said Regina roundly. "There isn't a particle of evidence for that tale, and I don't believe a word of it."

"But how can you dismiss Hayley's diary so lightly? One of my predecessors in office, Mr. Kenyon, the incumbent in the midseventeenth century, left a very circumstantial journal—"

"Your predecessor was a demented witch-hunter," objected Regina firmly. "He left a reputation, as well as a journal, and personally I think I'd rather be called a witch than the things some of his contemporaries called him. By all accounts he'd have had half the village searched and hanged if he'd had his way, but luckily the local justices knew him too well, and were pretty easygoing country fellows themselves, so he didn't do much damage. But *don't* quote him as evidence! No, Mr. Kenyon," she said, fixing Tom with a smiling but authoritative blue eye, "the occasional people who strayed into fairyland, or limbo, or whatever is inside magic mountains, I'll stand for. I don't mean they necessarily happened, these Rip Van Winkle vanishings, but I do accept that people here *believed* they happened. But witches, no! There never have been and there never will be any witches on the Hallowmount!"

And that was the sum of what he had got out of the evening, that and the fifteen minutes of unbelievable anguish and bliss on the way home, with Annet silent beside him in the passenger seat. That was the night he began to realize fully that this was different, that he couldn't make use of it and wasn't capable of disentangling himself from it; that he would never get over her, and never again be as he had been before he had known her. What he had thought to be a mild infatuation, only a little more serious than half a dozen others he had lived through and exploited, had grown and deepened out of knowledge, until it filled all his world with its new sensitivity, inordinately painful and disturbing. Annet was like that. He should have known at sight of her. But at sight of her it had already been too late to back away.

And then this afternoon, half-term Thursday. He had had a free last period, and got away early to pick up his case and set out on the drive home; and as he slid out of the car at the gate Annet had come out in her dark blue coat, a nylon rain scarf over her hair, three letters in her hand. At sight of him she had checked and recoiled very slightly, and the kind, careful, palpable veil of withdrawal had closed over her face. She knew his wants, and was sorry; she did not want him, and was a little sorry for that, too, or so it seemed to him. If she had not liked him she would have not troubled to evade him, she would not have shrunk from so small an encounter; but she liked him, and preferred not to have to remind him at every touch that she had nothing to give him that could ever satisfy him.

"You'll get wet," he said fatuously, "it's coming on to rain. Let me take them for you."

"I don't mind," she said. "I want a breath of air, I don't mind the rain."

"I'll run you down, then, at least let me do that."

"Thank you, but no, please don't. I just want to walk." She saw the next plea already quivering on his lips, and staved it off rapidly and gently. "Alone," she said, the deep voice making it an apology and an entreaty, while her eyes stood him off with the blue brilliance of lapis lazuli in an inlaid Egyptian head.

"I'm sorry!" she said. "Don't be hurt. I should only be horribly unsociable if you did come, and I'd rather not."

She had even gone to the trouble to find several small, kind things to say to him, she who had no small talk, softening her enforced rejection of him—and why had he forced it?—with reminders of his family waiting at home, of the long journey before him, and the advisability of making an early start and taking advantage of the remaining daylight to get as far as the M1. And he had followed her lead gratefully, glad to return to firmer ground.

"Your people must be looking forward so much to having you home again."

He said he supposed they probably were. What could he say?

"Have a pleasant journey! And a nice weekend!"

"Thank you! And you, too. See you on Tuesday evening, then. Good-bye, Annet!"

"Good-bye!"

She went up the lane toward the postbox outside the Wastfield gate. He went into the house, drank a hasty cup of tea, finished the packing of his single case, and set off again in the Mini toward Comerford.

And chancing to lift his eyes to the long, rain-dimmed hogback of the Hallowmount as he drove, just as the clouds parted and the quivering spear of light transfixed it, he saw the moving sapphire that was Annet climb the hillside and vanish over the crest.

CHAPTER 2

It was after eight o'clock on Tuesday evening when he lifted and dropped the knocker on the front door of Fairford, and listened with pricked ears to the footsteps that advanced briskly from the living room to open the door to him. He hadn't taken his key south with him. There were only two, and the whole family would be in on a Tuesday evening, so there was no question of his being locked out.

He said afterward that he knew as soon as the knocker dropped that something was wrong, but the truth was that the hole in his peace of mind really showed itself when he recognized the footsteps as belonging to Mrs. Beck. There was no reason in the world why that should be a portent of any kind; but we make our own superstitions and our own touch-stones, and it had been Annet who opened the door to him first, and she should have opened it to him now. If she had, he would have believed that he was being offered another chance, a new beginning with her, if he had the wit to make better use of it this time. But the steps were heavier and shorter than hers, the hand that turned back the latch was sharper and clumsier with it, and he knew Mrs. Beck even before she let him in.

"Ah, there you are, Mr. Kenyon!" She held the door wide. The hall was in half darkness; the brittle brightness of her voice might have been trying to make up for the want of light on her face. "Have you had a nice weekend?"

Had he? Back from a brief reinsertion into a vacancy which no longer seemed large enough for him, back to a desired but elusive right of domicile which had not yet fully admitted him, he couldn't find much comfort anywhere. But he said yes, he had, all the more positively for the nagging of his doubts. What else can you say? Everybody'd been almost overglad to see him, and made all the fuss of him even he could ever have wished; that ought to add up to a nice weekend, according to his old standards.

"We've missed you," said Mrs. Beck, making a production of taking his coat from him and hanging it up. He unwound his college scarf, and was stricken motionless for a second in midswing, arm ridiculously extended, at a statement so disastrously off-key. She didn't say things like that. She was too correct and practical, and they hadn't, so far, been on that kind of terms. It was then he began to feel the ground quake under him with certainty that something was wrong.

There was no Annet in the living room, no glossy black head lifting reluctantly from her book to speak faint, warm, rueful civilities over his return. Only Beck, with his glasses askew and his lofty brow seamed and pallid, almost mauve beneath the light. Too ready with a rush of welcoming conversation,

missing his footing occasionally in his haste, like his
wife. But unlike his wife, lurching at every misstep;
and his eyes, distorted by the lenses of his glasses,
liquefying at every recovery into anxiety and fear.

"Annet working late?" asked Tom, himself shaken
off course by this inexplicable disquiet.

If the pause was half a second long, that was all; if
they did exchange a look across his shoulder, it
touched and slid away in an instant.

"No," said Mrs. Beck, "she's gone into Comerbourne with Myra; there was some film they wanted
to see. One of these three-hour epics. They'd have to
miss the end if they caught the last bus, they'll stay
overnight with Myra's aunt in Mill Fields."

She must have seen his face fall, if she hadn't been
so busy desperately holding up her own. But he
accepted it; he swallowed it whole, and gave up
expecting to see Annet that night. Flat and cold the
evening extended before him; and if he hadn't suc-
cumbed to his hideous disappointment and taken
cravenly to flight from the prospect of keeping up
appearances face to face with her parents through
all those dragging hours, the course of events might
have been radically changed. But he did succumb,
and he did resort to flight. Better drive over to the
local club in Comerford than sit here trying to keep
his mouth from sagging. He made his excuses win-
ningly, and had the discomfiting sensation of having
hurled himself at an unlatched door when they
received them almost eagerly, without even formal
regret at being deprived of his company.

He withdrew himself thankfully as soon as supper
was over; he'd have skipped that, too, if he'd been
less hungry, or if there'd been much prospect of
getting a meal in Comerford at this hour. In the hall
he wound himself up again in his scarf, and then,

remembering that he was wearing his scuffed driving shoes, opened the large clothes cupboard to fish out some more presentable ones.

And suddenly something fell into place, a doubt, a premonition, a memory, whatever it was that put his own intended moves out of mind, and set him searching through the many coats on their hangers, looking for the dark gentian blue one with the large collar. Her best amber-gold one was there, the new one she had bought only a few weeks ago. Her second-best tweed raincoat was there. But not the blue. When did Annet ever go into town to the cinema in her everyday coat? He looked for the blue nylon head scarf, that she used to drape casually over the rail, since it could hardly be creased even if one tried. He couldn't find it. And her shoes, the shoes she had been wearing that rainy Thursday afternoon, strong half-brogue walking shoes suitable for such weather—where were they? Her more prized pairs she nursed carefully in her own room, but her walking shoes stayed down here. Where were they now?

Slowly he went back into the living room. They both looked up at him with a quick, oblique uneasiness, and fastening on his face, calmed and stilled into a kind of resigned despair.

"It's a fine night," he said, with what sounded even in his own ears like horrible inconsequence. "Stars shining, not a sign of rain. Did she go off wearing her rain hood, and her heavy shoes, a night like this?"

No one, apparently, noticed his effrontery in making deductions unasked about Annet's movements; no one bridled at his asking these questions as though he had a right to an answer. The Becks looked at each other with a long, drear look, and crumpled before his eyes.

"She isn't out with Myra—is she?"

"No," said Mrs. Beck, and straightened her back and met his eyes wretchedly; not resenting him, almost grateful for him. As a pair they only depressed and degutted each other, those two, they grasped at a third, now that it was inevitable, like drowning men at a good solid log. "No, she isn't." She dropped her hands in her lap, and let them lie, let the breath go out of her body in a great, helpless sigh.

Tom moistened his lips. "She went out on Thursday," he said, "just as I came in. She was wearing that blue coat she wears around, and those shoes, and the rain hood. That makes sense, it was raining then. But where I've been it hasn't rained again all the weekend. I don't know about here. But the roads were bone dry all the way."

"It hasn't rained here, either," said Mrs. Beck in the same flat, drearily angry tone. Beck made an inarticulate sound of protest, and she rode over him, raising her voice. "What's the use? He may as well know. At this rate everybody'll know before long. Where's the sense in thinking we can keep it quiet? She did go out on Thursday afternoon. She said she was going to post the letters and then have a quick walk before tea. She said she wouldn't be long."

"Mother!" said Beck in reproachful appeal. She turned her head for a moment and gave him a startled, wondering, almost derisive look in return for the incongruous word; but her eyes came back almost at once to Tom's face. If she was pinning her hopes to anyone at this minute, he realized, it was to him.

"And she never came home," said Mrs. Beck.

Once it was out they could all breathe and articulate again, and by an appreciable degree the tension eased. Things admitted can be faced. They have to be, there's no choice in the matter. But they were all trembling; and the relationship between them, that had been so decorous and neutral until that moment, would never be the same again.

Very carefully, so as not to unbalance himself and them, Tom asked, "Have you notified the police that she's missing?"

They had not. They shook their heads mutely, eyeing each other, each willing the other—he should have foreseen it—to tell him the reasons that were so obvious to them and should have been incomprehensible to him. They imagined him seeing Annet, with her perilous beauty, dead in a ditch; they couldn't know that he was seeing her rather as they saw her, alive, resolute and passionate, in the company of some other man. Or boy. Or whatever sixth-formers are these days, with their prodigiously advanced bodies and their struggling half-adult minds, so mutually hurtful, so impossible fully to reconcile. He almost went along with their instinct for concealment, and concealed his own knowledge; but then he shook off the temptation and slashed his way through to the truth. For what mattered was not their sensitivities but Annet's safety.

"I know about that last time," he said. "I know why you kept it quiet. But what does that matter, when she may be in trouble worse than that? Someone has to find her. And they've got the best chance, the best facilities. You'll have to go to them."

"Yes," said Beck, gray as cobwebs, "I suppose we shall. But you see, once before she went off of her own will—or tried to. And now again. People will say—they'll call her— We didn't want that. No more scandal round her name, not if we could avoid it. What will her life be like, if—? It's for her own sake!"

"And ours, too," said his wife flatly and coldly. "Because we know we're to blame, too. We're out of touch with her, we don't know how, we don't know why. We've no influence over her. But that makes it our fault as much as hers. Where did we fail? Where did we lose contact with her?" She turned her rigidly waved head and looked at Tom with fierce, helpless eyes. "Who told you? Are people still talking?"

"No. Not the way you mean. Someone told me rather with the opposite intention, to soften the effect if anyone else should gossip, that's all. But I can see that you hoped she'd just come home in her own good time, or write to you, and nobody else any the wiser. Did you *look* for her?"

A fool's question; or maybe a lover's, someone who can't trust anyone else to value his divinity or exert himself for her fittingly. Of course they'd looked for her. Beck had tramped the lanes and combed Comerford all the evening and half the night, and then gone off by bus to his sister's house in Ledbury, and his cousin's Teme valley smallholding, in case she had turned up there; Mrs. Beck had sat at home over the telephone, calling up with careful, ambiguous messages anyone who might, just might know anything, anyone who had a window overlooking the railway station, or a teenage son who could, in some way, be brought into the conversation and eliminated from the enquiry. But there were plenty of mothers of young sons with whom she wasn't on telephoning terms, plenty of dancing partners who didn't move in her orbit at all. And she had got nowhere.

"And Mrs. Blacklock? Hasn't she been on the line wanting to know where her secretary's got to?"

"Regina's away. She's been away all the weekend at some conference in Gloucestershire—something about child psychology. She gave Annet the whole week off. If Annet came back now, no one would know—no one but us three. Mrs. Blacklock won't be back until tomorrow night."

She offered that as a lifeline, and as such he clutched at it. Because if that was the case, Annet also might come back tonight, or tomorrow, in time to be stonily in her place when next Regina looked for her. That was if this was not final; if she meant it only as a fling, a gesture, a statement of her own will and her determination to go her own way. That was what her mother was hoping for, he saw that. Damage there would still be, irreparable after its fashion; but the worst damage is the known damage, and this, barring the last cruelty of fate, wouldn't be known. If he hadn't been so acutely tuned to everything that touched Annet, not even he need have known it.

"She's clever," said Mrs. Beck strenuously, "and strong-willed, and capable about practical things. She can take care of herself, and she's no fool. We thought she'd come home in time. We did what we could to find her ourselves, but we didn't want to start a hue and cry. If we did, she'd be ruined."

"You must see that," said Beck, pleadingly. He might have been an old man in his dotage, looking to his son to save something for him out of his life's wreckage.

"I do see it, I can understand it. But it's five days! And no message, no letter, nothing?"

"Nothing!"

"And what if it isn't what you think? Haven't you been afraid of that? What if she's come to some harm through no fault of her own, while we're writing her off as her own casualty? We've got to go to the police. What matters now is to find her."

Deliquescing, disintegrating before his eyes, they owned it. They dwindled, leaning on him. If he could bring her back safely and keep them their faces and their respectability through this they would give her to him gladly. Only he didn't want her given, he wanted her to come of her own will, as of her own will she had turned her back on him. All manner of perversity he read into her actions, but he would have cut off his own hand to have her back intact, whether she ever came his way or no.

"I saw her," he said deliberately. "Last Thursday, when I left. I was driving along the lane past the farm, and the sun came out on the Hallowmount. I saw Annet then. She was climbing up the side of the hill, toward the top. I saw her go over the crest and disappear. Do you know what she could have been doing there?"

Staring at him without comprehension, almost unbelievingly, they shook their heads. But even at that straw they clutched eagerly.

"Are you sure? Then she couldn't have been heading for the station, or the bus. And she had no luggage," said Mrs. Beck, her face flushing into life and hope again.

"Not with her then. But she could have left a small case somewhere to be collected." How could they, how could he, talk of her like that? Not some common little delinquent, but Annet, whose erect, flaming purity he saw now for the first time. And yet she was gone, and surely not alone. Why should she go at all, if she was alone? She knew very well how to seal up her solitude against all comers; she needed no distance between herself and men. But what could he do but go on fighting for her in these small, corrupt, prosaic, impertinent ways? She was in the world, they must reckon with the world if she would not.

"It was Miles Mallindine last time," he said. "At least I can go and see that he's safely at home this time. Bill won't mind my dropping in, I can make some excuse." They were on "Bill" terms then, he was welcome in their house whenever he dropped around, and they wouldn't know he was riding herd on their son, he'd see to that. Eve, who hadn't blamed the boy, wouldn't blame the girl too much, either. Eve had a fair, sweet mind. He wished Annet had had her for a mother, and Miles for a brother. There might have been no problem then.

"We ought to go to the Hallowmount," said Beck, astonishingly. And as they stared at him blankly, "She went there. It's the last we know of her. There might be something to speak to us. How can we be sure there isn't? We ought to go. At least to look where she went."

"We can look," said Tom without enthusiasm, for if there was one thing certain it was that they wouldn't find her there. Whatever she had wanted on that solitary hill, it was over long ago. Her case? But why there?

"Please! On our way to the Mallindines', it wouldn't take us long. There's a moon."

And they went, the two men together, in the light of the newly risen moon, whiter than daylight and almost as bright.

"You'll stay in the car at Mallindine's," said Tom firmly, rolling the Mini out onto the bone-white ribbon of the lane.

"Oh, yes, I will. They won't know." He would have promised anything. He was shaking like an old, old man. He loved his daughter, after all, or else he was sensible of some secret dismay of guilt, and heartily afraid.

"She was here," said Tom, calf-deep in the bleached autumn grass, panting from his climb. "When I first saw her, that is. About here. And she went on climbing on this line. Fast."

He climbed. The hogback of the hill heaved above him, white in the moonlight; here and there an encrustation of heather, but most of it pale, withered grass, dehydrated, dying. Like fair, tangled, luster-less hair. The night was still, starry above, bone naked in its pallor below. And yet a little curl of wind spiraled upward in front of his feet, coiling through the grass on the path Annet had taken up the steep. Coiling, twining, bending the strawy stems, just in front of his feet all the way. Some trick of displacement of air, alien humans intruding on the filled and completed spaces of the night. What else could it be? Or a small ground wind that never reached his knee. Or something light going before him, inviting, showing the way, itself unseen. Showing the right way, or the wrong?

Beck labored behind him, panting heavily, but he couldn't wait for him, the quivering of the grass drew him on, hypnotically, alluring. They had left the lower outcrop of rocks behind on their right hand, jagged in black and white like broken teeth. Against the skyline, faded periwinkle blue and faintly lumi-nous beyond that enormous moon, the tips of the rocks at the Altar just showed clear of the grass. At close quarters they stood thirty feet high, a horse-shoe shape with a worn space of grass enclosed in their uneven arms, a picnickers' delight. The ring of squat trees, stooping, misshapen pines half peeled of their bark, still lay out of sight on the summit.

He turned his head, and saw the bowl between the border hills drowned, drained of all color, a landscape solitary and strange as the craters of the moon. He withdrew his eyes from it with a wrench, and leaned into the slope as though his life, or a life incredibly becoming almost dearer than his own, depended on his reaching the top of the hill. Though there could be nothing here for them, nothing at all, no sign. If she had left her prints charmed into the grass, this acid whiteness of the moonlight would have bleached them all away.

There was a real wind up here, no longer a mysterious tremor that trod out the path for him, but a steady, light breeze that blew from behind him, from the hills of the west. So it was that he heard nothing as he breasted the last yards of the slope toward the Altar, panting, and saw suddenly before him the small, slender ankles moving in a rhythm of confidence and peace, the light feet furrowing the grasses. No color in the shoes, the stockings, only gradations of gray, no color in the narrow skirt gripping her thighs as she came. No color in the coat now, no gentian blue, only a deeper, dimmer gray, soft-textured, melting into the night. And within the hoisted collar the abrupt darkness of blue-black hair, the more abrupt whiteness and clarity of an oval face.

His eyes reached the face, and he had to halt and stiffen his legs under him to sustain the weight of relief and gratitude. Everything else could wait, the incipient rage, the anxiety that would surely close in again within minutes to impede all contact between them. What did they matter? He was looking at Annet. Annet, alive, intact and alone.

She came dropping down the slope toward them with her soft, lithe stride, not hurrying, not delaying, one hand in her pocket, one holding up her collar to her chin. He saw her face pale and still, with great eyes enormously dilated. She was aware of him; she saw them both, converging upon her, and knew them very well, and yet it seemed to him that she was looking through them rather than at them, that her mind and her heart were somewhere infinitely distant and inaccessible. He could not put a name to the disquiet she roused in him, or the quality of the pale, charged brightness that vibrated about her moonlit movements. But he knew he was frightened, that he dreaded the unavoidable questions to which he didn't want to know the answers. And all the time she was drawing nearer, her steps quickening a little; and there was no escaping the moment and the spark.

But when the spark flashed, Beck was breathless, and Tom was dumb. It was Annet who looked wonderingly from face to face, and asked in a voice shaken between offense and uneasiness, "What are *you* doing here? Is anything the matter?"

Was anything the matter! As though they had offended her by coming out to meet the last bus, as though they could not trust her to come home alone. The same erected head and faintly, gravely hostile face, unaware of having given more cause for anxiety than she did every day by being aloof and independent of them. Or was it quite the same? Her eyes were so wide and opaque and strange, as though she had only just awakened from sleep, and deep within the blankness a small, remote flame of disquiet kindled as he watched. But not fear; only disquiet, as though they were the unaccountable ones.

He said, "We came to look for you." What else could he say?

Still out of breath, her father said with feeble anger, "Where've you been? When you went out you said you'd be in to tea." Fantastic, the commonplaces that came most readily to the tongue; maybe wisely, for what could words do about it now?

"I know," said Annet, her voice almost conciliatory, something like a smile playing over her face for the absurdity of all this. "I meant to. I know I'm horribly late, I went a long way, farther than I realized. I couldn't believe it was so late, it seemed to drop dark all at once. But you didn't have to send out a search party, surely? I thought you'd be home by now, Mr. Kenyon. You didn't stay because of me, did you?"

And then she did smile, vaguely and sweetly and penitently, softened and eased by the night and the silence and that something in herself that kept her lulled and still like a dreaming woman; and the smile died on her lips and left them parted on held breath as she saw their fixed and wondering faces. Their own wariness, incomprehension and quickening fear stared back at them from her dilated eyes.

"What's the matter? I'm sorry I'm late, but why should you be alarmed about a couple of hours? I really don't see— I'm not even wet, it's stopped raining. What *is* the matter?"

Carefully, in a breathy voice that hurt his throat, Beck asked, "And what about the five days in between?"

She looked from one face to the other, and the smile was as dead as the skeleton rocks bleaching in the moonlight below them. She moistened her lips and tightened her grip on the raised folds of her collar. In the great dark eyes the little flames of fear burned high and bright.

"I don't know what you mean," said Annet in a thin whisper. *"What five days?"*

CHAPTER 3

He got up as soon as it was light, and dressed and went out. What was the point of staying in bed? He hadn't slept more than ten minutes at a stretch all night. He couldn't stop hearing her voice, patiently, desperately, wearily going over the recital time after time, unshakable in obstinacy.

"I went out to post the letters, and met Mr. Kenyon at the gate. He offered to take them for me, but I wanted some fresh air, so I walked. What else can I tell you? That's what I did. I went for a long walk, right over the Hallowmount and along the brook. I meant to come back round by the bog, but it got dark so quickly I changed my mind and climbed back over the top. And then I met them, and that's all. It's Thursday. Whatever you say, it must be Thursday, it was Thursday I went out with the letters. What's happened to you all?"

And the two of them at her, one on either side, frightened and angry but afraid to be too angry, afraid to drive her further from them; anxious, bit-

ter, piteous, throwing the same questions at her over
and over.

"Where did you go? Where did you spend the
nights? Who went with you? What's come over you?
Do you expect us to believe a fairy tale like that?"

He had driven them home, and then torn himself
away as inconspicuously as he could, but he hadn't
been able to help hearing the beginning of it. What
right had he in that scene? Annet didn't want or need
him, and he didn't want to hear them call her a liar.
He got out of the house, and took the car and drove
into Comerford. All the way along the quarter of a
mile of solitary, moonlit road, under the flank of that
naked slope, he was repeating to himself that at
least she was alive and well, and that was everything. Wherever she had been, whatever was the
truth about her lost five days, she was alive and
well, and home. But by the ragged, chaotic pain that
frayed him he knew that that was not quite everything. And he knew that she would win, that in the
end, true or not, they would all be committed to the
same uneasy silence and acceptance.

One thing he could do, and he did it. He parked
the Mini in the drive of Bill Mallindine's modern
house by the riverside, and made returning a borrowed book the excuse for his unexpected call. Eve
was out at some improbable feminine meeting, but
Bill gave him a drink and a chair by the fire, and
welcomed him gladly. And he hadn't even had to ask
any questions. At a table in one remote corner of the
multiple living room—heaven knew how they heated
it so successfully, the crazy shape it was—Miles
Mallindine and Dominic Felse were devotedly disentangling finished cassettes from cameras, and
securing them in their little yellow bags ready for
the post. Their heads together over the work, they

gave him the polite minimum of attention. It was Bill who teased Miles to display some of his best pictures, and volunteered the information that the two had spent the half-term camping and climbing near Tryfan. The two pairs of boots, bristling with triple hobs and clinkers, carelessly offloaded in the hall, should have spoken for themselves.

So that, as far as it went, was that. Miles was home, with enough paraphernalia to provide him with an alibi, and with a reliable ally to bear witness for him into the bargain. And if they'd really planned anything together, Annet and he, wouldn't they have taken care to cover her tracks as well as his?

And besides, there was the incredible conviction with which she had carried off her return, the dozen details that couldn't be shrugged away. The mention of her surprise at seeing him, when he should have been well on his way home, the reassurance that she wasn't even in danger of getting wet, because it had stopped raining, when it hadn't rained for five days. And her charmed, distant face, and the suddenly engendered fear and wonder as the ground shook under her feet. Could she, could anyone, act like that? It was hard to believe.

Almost as hard as that the earth had opened and admitted her into secret, terrible places, and given her back at the end of five days with no memory of the time between, not a minute older than she went away. Late, late in a gloaming Kilmeny had come home, all right, but whether from some fairy underworld or a cheap hotel God-knew-where, that was more than he dared guess. Bonny Kilmeny! She was that, whatever else she might be. And Kilmeny, you'll remember, he said to himself bitterly, driving home, was pure as pure could be. Who are you, to say Annet isn't?

It wasn't over when he got home. He had prayed that she'd be in bed, and her parents too exhausted to harrow the barren ground over again for him. But she was still there, and all that was changed was that the passion was clean gone out of her repeated affirmations, nothing left but the simple repetition of facts, or what she claimed were facts. She was indifferent now, she spoke without vehemence; if they believed her, well, if they did not, she couldn't help that. She was tired, but eased; and there was something still left in her face and body of a strange, rapt, content. The strongest argument for her, if she had but known it. They might plead, and argue, and lament; she had only to withdraw into her own heart, and she was secure from all troubling. He could feel the truth of that, at least. The source of warmth and joy and security was within her, some perfection remembered. Not remembered, perhaps, only experienced still. My God, but it couldn't be *true! Could it?*

And when they all said good night, like relatively civilized people, suddenly it was clear that they would speak no more of this. She could not be shaken. She could only be convinced by the production of a letter received in answer to one she had posted on Thursday, by the torn-off leaves of the calendar, and their collective certainty. Confronted with these, she shrank in bewilderment and fright, and from accusing they had to reassure her. Did any of them believe? Was it even possible to believe? Elsewhere he would not have credited it, but here on the borders the frontiers of experience grew generously wide and imaginative. They winced from pressing her too hard, probably they were grateful that they had not been able to catch her out in any particular. Wasn't it better to let well alone, and pray a little? Dreading, nevertheless, what revelation might yet erupt to confound them all.

Nobody knew! That was sanctuary, that nobody knew but the four of them, and please God, nobody ever would. He was so tangled into their household now that he would never get clear. Maybe he had drawn too close to Annet, in everything but blood, ever again to be considered as more distant than a brother.

Perhaps that was why he couldn't sleep, why he arose before dawn, and went like a sensible modern man to look over the ground by daylight. Painfully new daylight, but clear enough to show details the moon had silvered over. Because she must be lying. *(Mustn't she?)* And if she was lying, where had she been? Farther away than the other side of the Hallowmount. And what had she been doing? *(And with whom?* But that was the question he would not entertain; he pushed it out of sight as soon as it reared its head.)* Even granted the simple possibility of amnesia, she must have been somewhere. And from that somewhere she had returned precisely to the Hallowmount, as if only through the medium of that incalculable place could she reach her home again. That made this as surely a translation back from fairyland as if the earth had truly opened and let her go.

Again he climbed the hill, this time in the gray first light of a dull morning. Once over the crest he looked down upon the shallower undulations of another moorland valley, open heath grazing on both sides of the narrow brook that threaded it. An unpopulated, bare, beautiful desolation in changing tints of heather and bracken and furze. Not a single house in sight. No one here but sheep to stare at him and wonder as he dropped in long strides down the hill. On a wet Thursday afternoon there'd be no picnickers, no hill walkers, no one to watch Annet Beck disappear into the underworld. Not like venturing on to Comerbourne station with a suitcase in broad daylight, among hundreds of people who knew her. But if this was to be considered as an escape route to somewhere else instead of fairyland, then there had to be a means of leaving this bowl of wasteland, and faster than on foot. Footpaths were here by the dozen, trailing haphazard across the country from nowhere to nowhere, apparently, skirting the patches of bog where the cotton grass fluttered ragged and frayed. With a pony you could cover the ground here at a good speed, but Annet wasn't one of the local jodhpurs and 'ard 'at sorority, and with a pony she would in any case have been courting notice when she did encounter human beings. Could a car be got up here? He had been long enough in these parts now to realize that there were comparatively few places round these border uplands where the local people couldn't get cars to go. They had to; they lived in every corner of the back of beyond.

The long, oval, tilted bowl of pasture rose to northward, toward Comerford, and dipped to southward, in the direction of Abbot's Bale. Both were out of sight. In a tract of land without cover you could still be private here; all you needed was neutral colors and stillness, and you were invisible.

The easiest run out of the bowl would surely be toward Abbot's Bale. And beyond the brook, in the broad bottom of the valley, there sprang to life irresolutely a tiny, trodden path, that broadened and paled as it followed the ambling brook downward, until it showed bared stones through here and there, and had grown to the dimensions of a farm cart, with two deep wheel ruts, and the well-trodden dip where the horse walked in the middle. Where it tunneled through the long grass it dwindled again, but always to reappear. Where it passed close to the marshy hollows the bright emerald green of fine, lush turf invaded it. In the distance there was a gate across it, and beyond probably others. But gates can be opened. Most gates, anyhow. A motorbike could be brought up here with ease, even a small car, if you didn't mind a rough ride. And whoever had met Annet here and taken her away wouldn't be noticing a few bumps, or even a few scratches threatening his paint.

To Abbot's Bale, and from there wherever you liked, and no one in Comerford or Comerbourne any the wiser, for neither need be touched. Her everyday coat, a sensible rain scarf, no luggage: Annet had taken no chances this time. No one should suspect; no one should have any warning. Afterward? Oh, afterward the flood, the price, anything. What would it matter, afterward?

He jumped the brook and made his way along the cart track. Deep ruts on both sides of him, in places filled with the moist black mud of puddles that never dry up completely. Brown peat water deep between the tufted grasses, distant, solitary birds somewhere calling eerily. The hoof track on which he walked had been laid with stones at some time, and stood up like a little causeway, only here and there encroached upon by the richer grass. There seemed to be no traces of a car having negotiated this road recently. Nor had he heard any sound of an engine break the silence last night, when she returned, but that great hogback of rock had heaved solidly between, and might very well cut off all sound.

Five dry days, and a brisk wind blowing for three

of them; the ground was hard and well padded with thick, spongy turf. Only in the green places where the marsh came close would there be any traces to be found.

He came to the first of them, and the stony foundation of the track was broken there, and the ground had settled a little, subsiding into a softer green tongue of fine grass. Moisture welled up round the toe of his shoe, and he checked in mid-stride and drew his weight back carefully. The wheel ruts still showed cushioned and smooth on both sides; no weight had crushed them last night, or for many days previously. But in the middle of the path a single indentation showed, the flattened stems silvery against the brilliant green. Too resilient to retain a pattern of the tread, the turf had not yet quite recovered from the pressure of somebody's motorbike tires.

There was no doubt of it, once he had found it. He followed it along almost to the first gate, and found its tenuous line three times on the way, to reassure him that he was not imagining things. Nowhere was there a clear impression of the tread; for most of the way the path was firm and dry, and where the damp patches invaded it the thick grass swallowed all but that ribbon of paler green. But he knew now that he was not mistaken; someone had brought a motorcycle up here from the direction of Abbot's Bale no longer ago than yesterday. A motorcycle or a scooter; he couldn't be sure which.

The sun was well up, and he was going to be late for breakfast; they'd be wondering, next, what had happened to him! He turned back then, and scrambled up the slope toward the ring of trees.

Miles Mallindine had a Vespa. And however many young men had danced with and coveted Annet, there was no blinking the fact that Miles had already got himself firmly connected with her comings and goings once, and could hardly expect to evade notice when something similar happened for the second time. Others might be possibles, but he was an odds-on favorite.

But he'd been camping somewhere near Llyn Ogwen and climbing on Tryfan with Dominic Felse. Or had he? All the long weekend? With a Vespa he could cover that journey quite easily in a couple of hours. And would young Felse lie for him? Neither of them struck him as a probable liar, and yet he was fairly sure that for each other, where necessary, they would take the plunge without turning a hair.

If you want to know, he told himself with irritation, lunging down the westward side of the Hallow-mount, there's only one straightforward thing to do, and that's ask. Not other nosy people who *may* have seen something, not his friend who'll feel obliged to put up a front for him, but Miles himself. At least give him the chance to convince you, if there's nothing in it, and to get it off his chest if there is.

As if that was going to be easy!

It took him all morning to make up his mind to it; but in his free period at the end of morning school he sent for Miles Mallindine.

"You wanted to see me, sir?"

The boy had come in, in response to his invitation, jauntily and easily, brows raised a little; unable to guess why he was wanted, you'd have said, but long past the days of instinctively supposing any summons to the staff room to be a portent of trouble.

"Yes, come in and close the door. I won't keep you many minutes." They had the room to themselves for as long as they needed it, but the thing was to keep it brief and simple; and tell him nothing that wasn't absolutely essential. "You own a Vespa, don't you?"

"Yes, sir," said Miles, agile brows jumping again.

"Did you go up to Capel Curig on it this weekend?"

"Yes. It's a bit of a load, with two up and the tent and kit, but we've got it to numbers now." He was filling in the gaps, kindly and graciously, to avoid leaving the bald, enquiring "Yes" lonely upon the air between them. But he was wondering what all this was about, and testing out all possible connections in his all too lively mind.

"Spend the whole time up there? When did you leave? And when did you get back yesterday?"

"Oh, left about half past five on Thursday, I think, sir. I called round to pick up Dom first, and we did the packing at our place. We'd been in about half an hour when you looked in at home last night—just long enough for a wash and supper."

He didn't ask point-blank, "Why?" but the slight tilt of his head, the attentive regard of his remarkably direct and disconcerting eyes, put the same question more diplomatically; and a small spark deep within the eyes supplemented without heat, "And what the hell's it got to do with you, anyhow?" *"Sir!"* added the very brief, engaging and impudent smile he had inherited from his mother.

Tom was tempted to soften this apparently pointless and unjustifiable interrogation with a crumb of explanation, or at least apology; but the boy was too bright by far. To try to disarm him with something like, "I'm sorry if this makes no sense to you; but *if* it makes no sense, you've got nothing to worry about!"—no, it wouldn't do, he'd begin tying up the ends before the words were well out. No use saying pompously, "I have my reasons for asking." He knew that already; he was only in the dark at present as to

what they could be, and at the first clue he'd be off
on the trail. The fewer words the better. The more
abrupt the better. They took some surprising, these
days, but at least he could try.

"Did you take your Vespa out earlier on Thursday
afternoon? A trial run, maybe, if you'd been working
on her? Say—round through Abbot's Bale to the
track at the back of the Hallowmount?"

If Miles didn't know what it was all about now, at
least he knew the appropriate role for himself. He
had drawn down over his countenance the polite,
wooden, patient face of the senior schoolboy. It
fitted rather tightly these days, but he could still
wear it. Ours not to reason why; they're all mad,
anyhow. Ours but to come up with, "Yes, sir!" or,
"No, sir!" as required. The mask had an additional
merit, or from Tom's point of view an additional menace; from within its bland and innocent eye holes you
could watch very narrowly indeed without yourself
giving anything away.

"No, sir, I didn't. I had her all ready the night
before, there was no need to try her out."

"And you weren't round there yesterday, either?
Before you got home?"

"No, sir."

He waited, quite still but not now quite easy; he
was too intelligent for that. And something subtle
had happened to the mask; the young man—not even
the young man of the world—was looking through it
very intently indeed. Tom got up from his chair and
turned a shoulder on him, to be rid of the probing
glance, but it followed him thoughtfully to the window.

"I take it, sir, I'm not allowed to ask why? Why I
might have been there?" The voice had changed, too,
frankly abandoning the schoolboy monotone, and far

too intent now to be bothered with the experimental graces of sophistication that were its natural sequel.

"Let's say, not encouraged. But if you've told me the truth, then in any case it doesn't matter, does it? All right, thanks, Mallindine, that's all."

He kept his head turned away from the boy, watching the dubious sunlight of noon scintillating from the thread of river below the bridge. He waited for the door to open and close again. Miles had turned to move away, but nothing further happened.

After a moment the new voice asked, with deliberation and dignity, "May I ask one thing that does matter?" No "sir" this time, Tom noted; this was suddenly on a different level altogether.

"If you must."

"Has anything happened to Annet?"

It hit him so hard that the shock showed, even from this oblique view. He felt the blood scald his cheeks, and knew it must be seen, and felt all too surely that it was not misunderstood. This boy was dangerous; he used words like explosives, only half realizing the force of the charge he put into them. Has anything happened to Annet! My God, if only we knew! But the simpler implication was what he wanted answered, and surely he was owed that, at least. Even if he was the partner of her defection, lying like a trooper by prearrangement, and sworn to persist in his lies, that appeal for reassurance might well be genuine enough, and deserved an answer.

"I hope not," said Tom with careful mildness. "I certainly left her fit and well when I came out this morning."

He had his face more or less under control by then, the blush had subsided, and he would not be surprised into renewing it. He turned and gave Miles a quizzical and knowing look, calculated to

suggest benevolently that his preoccupation with
Annet, in the light of history, was wholly understandable, but in this case inappropriate, not to say
naïve. But the minute he met the leveled golden
brown eyes that were so like Eve's, he knew that if
anyone was involuntarily giving anything away in
this encounter, it wasn't Miles. He knew what he
was saying, and he'd thought before he said it.
Fobbing him off with an amused look and an indulgent smile wouldn't do. Shutting the door he'd just
gone to the trouble to open wasn't going to do anyone
any good.

Tom came back to his table, and sat down glumly
on a corner of it. "You may as well go on," he said.
"What made you ask that?" Even that fell short of the
degree of candor the occasion demanded. He
amended it quite simply to, "How did you know?" If
he was the lover, he had good reason to know, but no
very compelling reason to show that he knew; and if
he wasn't—well, they were all a bit uncanny round
here, so he'd said, cheerfully including himself.
Maybe Eve was a witch, and had handed on her
powers to him for want of a daughter.

"My mother had a telephone call on Thursday
evening," said Miles with admirable directness.
"From Mrs. Beck."

There couldn't have been much communication
between those two ladies during the last few
months; no wonder Eve's thumbs had pricked.

"She made some excuse about asking when the
Gramophone Club was starting its winter program.
But then she worked the conversation round to me,
and fished to know what I was doing over the
weekend. My mother told me when I came back last
night. I didn't think there was anything in it, actually, until you began asking—related questions. Oh,

you didn't give anything away," he said quickly,
forestalling all observations on that point. His head
came up rather arrogantly; the wide-open eyes
dared Tom to stand on privilege now. "My mother
can connect, you know. But so can others. And I
don't suppose our house was the only one she
phoned—if it's like that."

We ought to have known, thought Tom. In a small
place where everyone knows everyone else's business, where half the women compare notes as a
matter of course, we ought to have known it would
leak out. How could she hope to go telephoning
around the whole village and half Comerbourne,
without starting someone on a hot trail?

"No," he said flatly, "I'm afraid it wasn't."

"She wouldn't realize," said Miles generously. He
might not have occult powers, but he had a pair of
eyes that could see through Tom Kenyon, apparently, as through a plate-glass window. "My mother
had good reason to look under the mat—if you see
what I mean. But some of 'em don't need a reason,
they do it for love. And my mother doesn't talk. But
plenty of them do."

How had they arrived at this reversal? The kid
was warning him, kindly, regretfully, like an elder,
of the possible unpleasantness to come; warning him
as though he knew very well how deeply it could and
did concern him, and how much he stood to get hurt.
Without a word said on that aspect of the matter,
they had become rivals, meeting upon equal terms,
and equally sorry for each other.

It was high time to close this interview, before
somebody put a foot wrong and brought the house
down over them both. They had to go on confronting
each other in class for the best part of a year yet;
they couldn't afford any irretrievable gaffes.

"Too many," he agreed wryly. "But gossip without any foundation won't get them far. And I take it that you and I can include each other among the nontalkers, Mallindine."

"Yes, sir, naturally."

"Sir" had come back, prompt on his cue. This boy really wanted watching, he was a little too quick on the uptake, if anything.

"If there's anything you want to ask me, do it now. But I don't guarantee to answer."

"There's nothing, sir. If—" He did waver there, the elegantly held head turned aside for a moment; the eyes came back to Tom's face doubtfully and hopefully. "—if Annet's all right?"

"Yes, perfectly all right." He had nearly said, "Of course!" which would have been a pretense at once unworthy and unwise in dealing with this very sharp and dangerous intelligence. He dropped the attitude in time, but a faint, rueful smile tugged at Miles's lips for an instant, as if he had seen it hovering, and watched it snatched hastily away. The young man was back in charge, and formidably competent.

"Thank you, sir. Then that's all." For me it is, said the straight eyes, challenging and pitying; how about you?

"Right, then, off you go. And I shouldn't worry."

"Wouldn't you?" said the flicker of a smile again, less haughtily. Either Tom was beginning to see all sorts of shades of meaning that weren't there, or that last, long, thoughtful, level stare before the door closed had said, as plainly as in words: "Come off it! You know as well as I do there was another fellow in the case—nothing for you, nothing for me. Now tell me that doesn't hurt!"

He knew, as well as he knew his own name, that if he questioned Dominic Felse on the subject of the weekend in Wales, Dominic would go straight to Miles and report the entire conversation word for word; and yet it seemed to him that he had very little choice in the matter. Since he'd begun this probably useless enquiry, he couldn't very well leave an important witness out of it. He might be primed already, he might lie for his friend; but that was a hazard that applied to all witnesses, surely. And for some reason Tom felt sure that Miles would not yet have unburdened himself about that morning interview; he took time, when it was available, to think things out, and he had himself been considerably disturbed. He might not keep it quiet, but he wouldn't run to confide it until he knew what he wanted to say.

So Tom sent for Dominic Felse, half against his conscience and a little against his will, but already launched and incapable of stopping. Dominic confirmed that he and Miles had spent all the weekend together. Yes, they'd packed up together and left about half past five, maybe a little earlier. No, they hadn't been separated at all during the whole trip, except for half-hour periods while Miles took the scooter and went shopping, and Dominic cooked. Miles was no good as a cook. Yes, they'd come straight back to the Mallindines' for supper.

Why?

Dominic was nearly a year younger than Miles, and less impeded by his dignity and sophistication from asking the obvious questions. Moreover, he was the son of a detective-inspector, and had a consequent grasp of the rights of the interrogated which made him an awkward customer to interrogate. With sunny politeness he answered questions, and with reciprocal interest asked them. Tom got rid of him in short order, for fear of giving away more than he got.

He met the two of them in the corridor as he left when afternoon school ended. They gave him twin civilized smiles, very slight and correct, and said, "Good night, sir!" in restrained and decorous unison.

The sight of the two of them thus, shoulder to shoulder, with similarly closed faces and impenetrable eyes, settled one thing. They had pooled everything they knew, and were preparing to stand off the world from each other's back whenever the assault threatened.

He had seen it coming, and he didn't make the mistake of thinking that either of them would as lightly confide in a third party. All the same, he began to regret what he had set in motion. Would it really do any good to find out what had happened, and who had made it happen? Wasn't it better to creep through the next few days and weeks with fingers crossed and breath held, walking on tiptoe and praying to know nothing—not to have to know anything—like Beck and Mrs. Beck? Thankful for every night that closed in with no trap sprung and no revelation exploding into knowledge; frightened of every contact in the street and every alarm note of the telephone, but every day a little less frightened.

Annet came and went with fewer words than ever, but with a tranquil face. Something of wonder still lingered, and something of sadness and deprivation, too, and sometimes her eyes, looking through the walls of the house and the slope of the Hallowmount into whatever underworld she had left behind there, burned into a secret, motionless excitement that never seemed quite to be able to achieve joy. She went to Cwm Hall in the morning, and Regina

Blacklock's chauffeur drove her home in the evening, and nobody there seemed to notice anything wrong with her or her work. Thank God that was all right, anyhow! There were bushels of Regina's notes from the conference to decipher and type out, and a long report to her committee, which Annet brought home to copy on Thursday evening. On the incidence and basic causes of delinquency in deprived children!

She was working on it when Tom came through the hall after supper to go out and stable the Mini for the night. He heard the typewriter clicking away in the dingy little book-lined room Beck still called his study, though all he ever did in it was accumulate endless random text notes of doubtful value on various obscure authors, with a view to publishing his own commentaries someday. No one believed it would ever be done, not even Beck himself; no one believed the world stood to gain or lose anything, either way.

Tom opened the door gingerly and looked in, and she was alone at the desk. It was the first time he had been alone with her, even for a moment, since her return. He went in quickly, and closed the door softly at his back.

"Annet—"

She had heard him come. She finished her sentence composedly before she looked up. He could see no hardening in her face, no wariness, no change at all. She looked at him thoughtfully, and said nothing.

"Annet, I want you to know that if there's anything I can do to help you, I will, gladly. I'd like to think you'd ask me."

She sat and looked at him for a long moment, looked down at her own hands still poised over the keys, and back slowly to his face. He thought he caught the bleak, small shadow of a smile, at least a shade of warmth in her eyes.

"You'd much better just go on thinking me a liar," she said without reproach or bitterness. "It's nice of you, but I really don't need any help."

"I hope you won't, Annet. Only I'm afraid you may. I know, I feel, it isn't over. And I don't want you to be hurt."

"Oh, *that* doesn't matter!" said Annet, startled into a rush of generous words. "Not at all! You mustn't worry about me."

She smiled at him, the first real, unguarded smile he had ever had from her. If she had asked him to believe in fairyland then, he would have done it; any prodigy he would have managed for her. But the moment was over before it was well begun; for it was at that instant that the knocker thudded at the front door.

He shivered and froze at the sound. Annet's smile had grown suddenly, mockingly bright. "It'll be Myra, coming for me," she said, quite gently. "What are you afraid of?"

But it wasn't Myra. They heard Mrs. Beck cross the hall, quick, nervous steps, running to ward off disaster. They heard the low exchange of words; a man's voice, quiet and deep-pitched, and Mrs. Beck's fluttering tones between. He was in the hall now; only a few steps, then he was still, waiting.

The door opened upon Mrs. Beck's white, paralyzed face and scared eyes.

"Annet—there's someone here who wishes to speak to you."

He came into the doorway at her shoulder, a tall, lean man with a long, contemplative face and deceptively placid eyes that didn't miss either Tom's instinctively stiffening back or Annet's blank surprise.

"I'm sorry to interrupt your work, Miss Beck," said Detective-Inspector George Felse gently, "but there's a matter on which I'm obliged to ask you some questions. And I think, in the circumstances, it should be in your parents' presence."

CHAPTER 4

From the very first she seemed startled and bewildered, but not afraid; a little uneasy, naturally, for after all, George Felse was the police, and clearly on business, but not at all in trouble with her own conscience.

"Of course!" she said, and slid the bar of her typewriter into its locked position, and stood up. "Shouldn't we go into the living room? It's more comfortable there."

"But Mr. Kenyon—" began Mrs. Beck helplessly, and let the words trail vaguely away. An old, cold house, where was the paying guest to sit in peace if they appropriated the living room?

"That's all right," said Tom, torn between haste and unwillingness, "I'll get out of the way."

But he didn't want to! He had to know what he had let loose upon her, for he was sure this was his work. He should have let well alone. Why had he had to question Mallindine, and then go on to confirm what he well knew might still be lies by dragging in Dominic Felse? They'd compared notes almost be-

fore his back was turned; and young Felse had
promptly gone home and let slip the whole affair,
with all its implications, to his father. How else
could you account for this?

But no, that wouldn't do; as soon as he paused to
consider he could see that clearly. If Dominic had
informed on Annet, it was because something else
had happened during that lost weekend, something
that could be linked to a strayed girl and an improbable fairy story. Something of interest to the police,
whose sole interest in a pair of eighteen-year-old
runaways would be to restore them to their agitated
parents, and let the two families settle it between
them as best they could, and even that only if their
aid had been sought in the affair. No, there must be
something else, something that had frightened Dominic with its implications, and caused him either to
blurt out what he knew unintentionally, or driven
him to deliver it up as a burden too heavy and a
responsibility too great to be borne.

"It's just possible," said George Felse, eyeing him
amiably but distantly from beyond the rampart of his
official status, all the overtones of friendship carefully excised from a voice which remained gentle,
courteous and low-pitched, "that I may need to see
you for a few moments, too, Mr. Kenyon, if you
wouldn't mind being somewhere available, in case?"

He said he wouldn't, numbly and reluctantly, and
turned to go up to his own room. He didn't hurry,
because he wanted to be called back, not to be
excluded. In a way he would have given anything
to escape, but since there wasn't going to be any
escape, anyhow, and he had already been dragged
into the full intimacy of the family secret, what point
was there in putting off the event? And before he had
reached the stairs Beck was there, framed in the

doorway of the living room, wispy and gray and frightened, and looking desperately for an ally.

"What is it? Did I hear you say you want to talk to Annet, Mr. Felse?" His eyes wandered sidelong to Tom, who had looked back. "No, no, don't go, Kenyon, this can't be anything so grave that you can't hear it. Please, I should be glad if you'd stay. One of the household, you know. That's if you have no objection to being present?"

Panic gleamed behind the thick lenses of his glasses; not for anything would he be left alone with Annet and his wife and the threat George Felse represented. His wife would expect him to spread a male protective barrier between his womenfolk and harm; or she would not expect it, but watch his helplessness with a bitter, contemptuous smile, and that would be worse. And Annet would act as though he was not there, knowing she had to fend for herself. No, he couldn't do without Tom. He laid a trembling hand on his arm, and held him convulsively.

"It's rather if Felse has no objection," said Tom, watching the C.I.D. man's face doubtfully.

"No, this is not official—yet. Later I may have to ask you to make a formal statement. That will depend on what you have to tell me."

He was looking Annet in the eyes, without a smile, but with the deliberate, emphatic gentleness of one breaking heavy matters to a child. He had known her since she was a small girl with pigtails; not intimately, but as an observant man knows the young creatures who grow up round him in his own village, the contemporaries of his own sons and daughters. He'd had to pay similar visits to not a few of their homes in his time; he knew all the pitfalls crumbling under their uncertain feet.

"I'll tell you what I can," said Annet, brows drawn close in a frown of bewilderment. "But I don't know what you can want to ask me."

"So much the better, then," he said equably, and followed her into the living room, and turned a chair to the light for her. She understood that quite open maneuver, and smiled faintly, but acquiesced without apparent reluctance. The parents hovered, quivering and silent. Tom closed the door, and sat down unobtrusively apart from them.

"Now, Annet, I want you to tell me, if you will, how you spent last weekend."

George Felse sat down facing her, quite close, watching her attentively but very gently. If he felt the despairing contraction of the tension within the room he gave no sign, and neither did she. She tilted back her head, shaking away the winged shadow of her hair, as if to show him the muted tranquility of her face more clearly.

"I can't tell you that," she said.

"I think you can, if you will." And when she had nothing to say, and her mother only turned her head aside with a helpless, savage sigh, he pursued levelly: "Were you here at home, for instance?"

"They say not," said Annet in a small, still voice.

"Let them tell me that. I'm asking you what *you* say."

"I can only tell you what I told them," said Annet, "but you won't believe me."

"Try me," he said patiently.

She looked him unwaveringly in the eyes, and took him at his word. Again, in the same clipped, bare terms she retold that fantastic story of hers.

"Mrs. Blacklock gave me practically a whole week off, from Thursday morning, because she was going to the child-care conference at Gloucester. She

asked me to come in again on Wednesday—
yesterday—and clear up any routine correspondence, and then she came home in the evening. So I
had five free days. I hadn't made any plans to do
anything special. I meant to go to choir practice on
Friday night, as usual. Maybe to the dance on
Saturday, but I hadn't decided, because Myra was
going with a party to the theater in Wolverhampton,
so I hadn't anyone to go with. They must have
missed me at choir practice, and at church on
Sunday. If I'd intended not to be there, shouldn't I
have let them know?"

"He rang up on Friday night," said Mrs. Beck, a
little huskily. "Mr. Blacklock, I mean—after choir
practice. He was worried because she didn't turn
up, wondered if she wasn't well. I told him she had a
bit of a cold. He was quite alarmed, and I had to put
him off, or he'd have been round to see her. I said it
was nothing much, but she was in bed early, and
asleep, so he couldn't disturb her, of course. He rang
again on Sunday morning, after church, to ask how
she was."

"He only has four altos," put in Beck with pathetic
eagerness. "And she never lets them down. Mr.
Blacklock knows he can always rely on Annet for his
alto solos."

Annet's clenched lips quivered in a brief and wry
smile. It was all a part of the well-meaning commu-
nal effort to keep Annet busy and amused, everyone
knew that. The Blacklocks had been taken into Mrs.
Beck's embittered and indignant confidence, after
that abortive affair with Miles Mallindine, and with
her usual competence Regina had stemmed every
gap in the fence of watchful care that surrounded the
girl, and poured new commitments into every empty
corner of her days. Probably the choir was one of the

things she'd enjoyed most. Regina couldn't sing a note; it was Peter, with his patient, fastidious kindness, who manipulated the casual material at his disposal into a very fair music for a village church. No wonder he rejoiced in Annet's deep, lustrous, boy's voice. And as charged by his wife, he always brought or sent her home in the car; that was a part of his responsibility. If Annet ever defected again, it mustn't be while she was in their charge.

"So from Thursday morning you were free," said George mildly, undistracted by these digressions. "What did you do with your freedom?"

"I was home all Thursday afternoon. I washed some things, and played a few records, and wrote one letter. And my mother had two more to post, so about half past three I said I'd go and post them, and then go for a walk. I said I'd be back to tea. I met Mr. Kenyon just at the gate, and he offered to post the letters for me, but I told him I wanted some air and was going for a walk. It was just beginning to rain, but I didn't mind that, I like walking in the rain. I posted the letters in the box by the farm, and then I went on up the lane and over the stile on to the Hallowmount. I climbed right over the hill and went down into the valley by the brook, on the other side. I remember coming to the path there, this side the brook. I can't remember how much farther I walked. I can't remember noticing which way I went, or when it stopped raining. But suddenly I realized it was dark, and I turned back. It wasn't raining then. I thought I'd better get home the shortest way, so I climbed over the hill again, and there the grass was quite dry, and so were my shoes, and the moon was out. And just below the rocks there I met Mr. Kenyon and my father, coming to look for me. They *said* they were looking for me. It seemed silly to me.

I thought I was only a couple of hours late. But they said it was Tuesday," she said, eyes wide and distant and grave confronting George Felse's straight regard. "They said I'd been gone five days. I didn't believe it until we got home, and there was a letter for me, an answer to the one I'd posted. But I couldn't tell them any more than I've told you now, and I know they don't believe me. All the weekend, they say, they've been trying to find me, and covering up the fact that I wasn't here."

George sat silent, studying her thoughtfully for a moment. Nothing of belief or disbelief, wonder or suspicion, showed in his face; he might have been listening to a morning's trivialities from Mrs. Dale. Annet knew how to be silent, too. She looked back at him and added nothing; she waited, her hands quite still in her lap.

"You met no one on the hill? Or along by the brook?" It was hardly likely on a rainy Thursday afternoon, but there was always the possibility.

"No."

"Mr. Kenyon saw her," said Mr. Beck quickly.

"I was driving back along the lane about four," confirmed Tom, "on my way home for the weekend, and I happened to look up at the Hallowmount just as the sun came out on it. I saw her climbing toward the crest, just as she says."

"Could you be sure it was Annet, at that distance?"

"I'd seen her go out; I know just what she was wearing." Carefully he suppressed the aching truth that he would have known her in whatever clothes, by the gait, by the carriage of her head, by all the shape and movement that made her Annet, and no other person. "I was sure. Then, when I got back here on Tuesday evening, and found she'd been missing all that time, I told Mr. and Mrs. Beck about it, and we went there on the off-chance of picking up any traces. We didn't expect anything. But we found her."

"She was surprised to see us," said Beck eagerly. "She asked what we were doing there, and if anything was the matter. She said she knew she was very late, but surely we didn't have to send out a search party."

"She was particularly surprised to see me," added Tom. "She said she thought I should have been home by then, and surely I didn't stay behind because we were worried about her."

They were all joining in now, anxiously proffering details of the search for her, of her return, of the terrible consistency of her attitude since, which had never wavered. George listened with unshakable patience, but it was Annet he watched. And when he had everything, all but those tire tracks of which her parents knew nothing, and which Tom must mention only privately if he mentioned them at all, it was still to Annet that he spoke.

"So you went up the Hallowmount," he said, "and vanished out of time and place, like Tabitha Blount in the seventeenth century. And came back, also like Tabby, sure you'd been there no more than an hour or two, and never strayed out of this world. She never could give any account of her fairyland. Can you do any better?"

"I know I was happy," said Annet, disregarding all but what she wished to hear; and suddenly the blue eyes deepened and warmed into such a passion of triumph and anguished joy that George was startled and moved. "Happy" was a large word, but not too large for the blaze that lit her for a moment.

"There's nothing more you wish to tell me? And nothing you want to amend? It's up to you, Annet."

"There's nothing else I can tell you," she said. "I told you that before I began. Ask them if I've changed anything. I told you they didn't believe me. I can't help it if you don't believe me, either."

"I don't," said George simply. "Nor do I believe that your parents or Kenyon here have accepted it, never for a moment. Your missing five days were spent somewhere. As you very well know. I think, though I may be wrong, that you also know very well where, in every detail. I strongly advise you to think again, and tell me the truth, as in the end you'll have to."

Her father was at her side by this time, feebly fumbling her cold hand. Her mother was close on her left, gripping the arm of the chair.

"Mr. Felse, you must allow for the possibility of—of— More things in heaven and earth, you know— How can we presume to know everything?" Beck was tearing sentences to shreds in his nervousness, and dropping the tatters wherever they fell.

"She's been utterly consistent," Tom pointed out, trampling the pieces ruthlessly. Someone had to sound sane, and put the more possible theories. "I don't argue that you should believe in fairies—but you'll notice that Annet hasn't asked you to. She's made no claim at all that anything supernatural ever happened to her. She says she doesn't remember anything between going over the crest of the Hallowmount and coming to herself to realize it had grown dark, and then hurrying toward home. There's nothing fantastic about that. It doesn't happen often, but it happens, you know of cases as well as I do. Of course those five days were spent somewhere, we know that. But it may very well be true that Annet doesn't know where."

"Amnesia," said Mrs. Beck, too strenuously, and recoiled from the theatrical impact of the word, and said no more.

Why were they arguing like this, what was it they were trying to ward off? What did the police care about a truant weekend, provided no laws had been broken?

"It was a fine, dry weekend," said George reasonably. "About ten percent of the Black Country must have been roaming the border hills on Saturday and Sunday, and the odds are pretty good that a fair proportion of them were on the Hallowmount. They couldn't all miss a wandering, distressed girl. If any locals had seen her they'd have spoken to her. Everyone knows her. And did she reappear tired, hungry, anxious or grimy? Apparently not. She came down to you completely self-possessed, neat, tidy and fresh, asking pertinent questions. From fairyland, yes, perhaps. From amnesia one's return would, I fancy, be less coherent and coordinated."

He hitched his chair a little nearer to Annet; he reached and took her hands, compelling her attention.

"I don't doubt the happiness, Annet," he said gently. "In a way I think you've told me a kind of truth, a partial truth. Now tell me the rest while you can. You were no nearer the underworld than, say— Birmingham. Were you?"

Hard on the heels of the brief, blank silence, Beck said, in a high, hysterical voice, "But what does it mean? What if she actually was in Birmingham? That's not a crime, however wrong it may be to lie to one's family. What are all these questions *about?* I think you should tell us."

"Perhaps I should. Unless Annet wants to alter her story first?"

"I can't," said Annet. Braced and intent, she watched him, and whether it was incomprehension he saw in her face or the impenetrable resolution to cover and contain what she understood all too well, he still could not determine.

"Very well. You want to know what the questions are about. Last Saturday night, around shop-closing time," said George, "a young girl was seen, by two witnesses independently, standing on the corner of a minor—and at that hour an almost deserted—street in Birmingham. She was idling about as though waiting for someone, about forty yards from a small jeweler's shop. The first witness, an old woman who lives in the street, gave a fair description of a girl who answers very well to Annet's general appearance. The second one, a young man, gave a much more detailed account. He spoke to her, you see, wasted five minutes or so trying to pick her up. He described her minutely. Girls like Annet can't, I suppose, hope to escape the notice of young men."

"But however good a description you had," protested Tom, "why a girl from Comerford, of all places, when this was in Birmingham?"

"A good question. I'm coming to that."

"I suppose your son told you Annet was missing during the weekend," said Tom, bitterly and unwisely.

George gave him a long, thoughtful glance from under raised brows.

"No, Dominic's told me nothing—but thanks for the tip. No, the Birmingham police came to us because this girl, according to her unwelcome cavalier, was filling in the time while she waited, as one does, by fishing the forgotten bits out of her pockets.

Everyone has an end of pencil, or a loose lucky farthing, or a hair grip, or something, lost in the fluff at the seam. This girl had a bus ticket. She was playing with it when he accosted her, and she was nervous. That amused him. He paid particular attention to the way she was folding it up into a tiny fan—you know?—narrow folds across in alternate directions, then fold the whole thing in the middle. When he was too pressing—though of course he doesn't admit that—she drew back from him hastily, twisted the fan in her fingers and threw it down. He says he left her alone then. If she didn't want him, he could do without her. But when they took him back to the corner next day he knew where the ticket had lodged, close under the wall, in a cranny of paving stones. And sure enough, they found it there, and he identified it positively.

"It turned out," said George flatly, "to be a one-and-fourpenny by Egertons' service between Comerbourne and Comerford. With that and the description it wasn't so hard to settle upon Annet, once they came to us. Unfortunately no one saw the person for whom she was waiting. She told the youngster who accosted her she was waiting for her boyfriend, and he was an amateur boxer. So he didn't hang around to put it to the test."

"But what of it?" persisted Beck feverishly. "Why are they hunting for this girl—whoever she may be?"

"Because, around midnight that night, when a policeman on the beat came along, he saw that the steel mesh gate over the jeweler's doorway wasn't quite closed. All the lights in the shop were off, the gate was drawn into position, but when he tried it he found it wasn't secured. And naturally he investigated. He found the till cleared of cash, and several glass cases emptied, too, apparently of small jewelry.

The loss is estimated at about two thousand pounds, mostly in good rings.

"And the proprietor—he was an old, solitary man, who lived over his shop—he was in his own workroom at the back. His head had been battered in with a heavy silver candlestick," said George, his voice suddenly hard, deliberate and cold. "He was dead."

The gasp of realization and horror that stiffened them all jerked Annet for the first time out of her changeling calm, and out of her chair. She was torn erect, rigid, her face convulsed, her hands clutching at the empty air before her. The great eyes dilated, fixed and blank with shock. The contorted mouth screamed, "No—no,—*no!*" and her voice shattered on a suffocating breath.

Tom sprang wildly toward her, but it was George Felse who caught and lifted her in his arms as she fell.

CHAPTER 5

"Call her doctor," said George, over the limp, light body. "I'd rather he was here."

He put off Mrs. Beck, who was clawing frantically at her darling and spilling unwonted and painful tears, with a lunge of one shoulder, and carried his burden to the couch. "Tom, you get him. Use my name, he'll come all the quicker."

Tom got as far as the telephone before he realized that he did not even know which doctor they favored, and there being no emergency notes on the scratch pad to enlighten him, he was forced to come and drag Beck away from the couch to supply the information he needed. Annet was lying motionless and pale by then, a pillow under her cheek, her body stretched carefully at ease, the narrow skirt drawn down over her knee, surely by George Felse. Tom dialed with an erratic finger, hating George more for his deftness and humanity even than for his official menace. What right had he? What right? To strike her down, and then to be the one who held her in his

arms, and laid her down so gently among the cushions, and stroked back the tumbled hair from her
eyes with such assured fingers.

"Dr. Thorpe? I'm speaking for Mr. Beck at Fairford. Can you come out here at once, please? Yes,
it's urgent. Miss Beck—Annet—she's in a faint.
Detective-Inspector Felse is here, he told me to ask
you to hurry. I don't know—a degree of shock, I
suppose—he urges you to come as soon as possible.
Good, thank you!"

He hung up, and his hand was shaking so that the
receiver rattled in the rest. He went back to the
living room with Beck clinging close on his arm.

Mrs. Beck had control of herself again; the traces
of her few and angry tears mottled her cheeks, her
ruled dark hair, dull from many tintings, was shaken
out of its customary severity, but she was herself
again, and would not be overwhelmed a second time.
George had withdrawn and left Annet to her; not, it
seemed, from any embarrassment or incompetence
on his own part, rather to provide her with something urgent and practical to do, for he did not
withdraw far, and he watched her ministrations with
a close and somber regard.

"Is she subject to fainting fits?"

"I've never known her faint before." She gave him
a furious look over her daughter's body. "You frightened her. You shocked her."

"She could have read most of the same details in
tonight's paper," said George, "but I doubt if they'd
have had the same effect. She wouldn't have realized
then what she knows now—that it happened forty
yards away from her, while she was waiting for
her—friend. There are things she knows that I didn't
have to tell her. Such as where he was while she
stood waiting for him. If he'd been round the other

corner in the tobacconist's, buying cigarettes, I think Annet would have stood the shock of an unknown old man's death without collapsing."

"But, good God!" protested Tom, twisting away from the thought, "you're making out that she kept watch for him on the corner while he did it."

"That's one possibility. There are others."

He didn't go into them. He stood looking down at the pale, motionless face on the cushions, pinched and blue at the corners of the closed lips, a strange, faint frown, austere and distant, clenched upon her black brows. The silken wings of her hair spread blue-black on either side, buoyed up on the resilient down of the pillow like a drowned girl's hair afloat on water.

So slight, and so remote; and so incalculable. Was it possible to know her so well that she would someday be able to take down all the barriers and be relaxed and at peace with you? He'd never had much close contact with her. It might be only that unbelievably touching beauty of hers that made him feel her exile from her fellow men to be something imposed from without, and not chosen. That, and her age. She could have been Dominic's year-older sister. He would have liked a girl. So would Bunty, but there'd just never been one. Did she remain closed like an ivory box with a secret spring even when she was with X? Or open like a flower to the sun? The inescapable X. X who must be found, because he had almost certainly killed a solitary, eccentric, miserly old man for the contents of his till and the sweepings of three showcases.

"You haven't proved she was even there," said Beck, stirred to the feeble man's desperate bravery. "There must be many girls who fit the same description equally well. You see Annet's ill. She never faints. She was wandering somewhere all the week-end, and she's ill and frightened, and you have to use her so brutally."

"I'm sorry if you think I was brutal. I don't think I was guilty singlehanded of cutting the ground from under Annet's feet. Someone else did that. When he hit the old man. No," he said, looking down bitterly at the slow, languid heave and fall of Annet's breast, "I haven't proved she was there. I haven't proved she was the girl on the corner. I didn't have to. Annet told us that, pretty plainly. The only thing she has told us yet."

But it wasn't; not quite. She had told him, however unwillingly, the depth and height and hopelessness and helplessness of the love that was eating her alive. If they hadn't seen it, if they had no means of measuring or grasping it, that was their failure; and it looked as if that inadequacy in them might yet be the death of Annet. A little honest brutality might have cheered and warmed her, and brought her close enough to confide.

He looked up and caught Tom Kenyon's eye upon him. There was one who wasn't going to dispute his contention that Annet had betrayed herself. He'd wanted a reaction from her, and he'd got it at last, and it identified her only too surely.

"But you realize, don't you," said Tom with careful quietness, "that she's absolved herself, too? Oh, I know! If it wasn't Annet your witnesses saw, why should this be such a shock to her? But since it *is* such a shock, she *can't have known*. Can she? She can't have known anything about the murder, maybe not even about the robbery. She was there, yes, but quite innocently, waiting for him. She thought he was buying something, maybe a present for her. It was only because of their joint escapade that she wouldn't admit where she'd been. To keep him out of trouble, yes, but not *that* trouble—because she knew nothing about that until you just told her. Why else should it drop her like a shot?"

George said, "You make a pretty good case. If this is genuine, of course."

"*If* it's genuine! My God, man, look at the poor kid!"

No need to tell him that, he'd hardly taken his eyes off her. But he didn't commit himself to any opinion about the nature of this collapse. He'd been in the world and his profession long enough to know that deception has many layers, and women know the deepest of them. No question of Annet's unconsciousness now, no doubt of her anguish; but he had known self-induced illnesses and self-induced collapses before, as opportune as this, as disarming as this, sometimes even deceiving their victims and manipulators. When you can't bear anymore, when you want the questioning to stop, when you need time to think, you cut off the sources of reason and force and light, and drop like a dead bird off its roost in a frosty night. And as long as you stay darkened and silenced, no one can torment you.

Annet remained dark and silent a disquietingly long time. Cold water bathing her forehead brought no flicker to her pinched face.

"We'd better get her to bed," her mother said. "Arthur, help me with her."

"I'll carry her upstairs for you."

George stooped and slid an arm under the girl's shoulders, very gently easing her weight into balance against his breast. Her head rolled limply upon his shoulder, the black wing of glossy hair swung, and hid her face. Inside the loose collar of her yellow sweater a narrow thread of black velvet ribbon lay uncovered against the honeyed pallor of her neck. It moved with her weight, dipping between her little breasts.

He held her cradled against him, and ran his fingers round her neck beneath the fragrant drift of hair. There was a neat little bow tied there in the ribbon; he eased it round until he could untie it, and she never stirred, not even when he laid the loosened ends together, and drew out the treasure she had concealed between her breasts.

He held it out for them all to see, dangling on its ribbon: a narrow circlet of gold, a brand-new wedding ring.

They were upstairs with her a long time, the mother and the doctor, but they came down at last. George, who had sat all the time looking down with a shadowed face and dangling the ring by its ribbon, rose to meet them. He could think of nothing in his life that had filled him with so deep a sense of shame as the act of filching that tiny thing from her while she lay senseless; the most private and precious thing she possessed, the symbol of everything she wanted, and he could not let her keep it. He weighed it in his hand, and it was heavier than it should have been with all the inescapable implications that clung to it.

The old man's assistant, who had left him just preparing to lock up on Saturday night, had made an inventory of the stolen pieces, as far as his memory served him. There was no question as to whether he would be able to identify the ring; a tiny private mark was scratched beside the assay marks inside it; whoever had had it in his stock would know it.

"Has she come round?"

"How is she?"

Two of them asked together; Arthur Beck, suddenly piteously old and withered, only trembled and waited.

"Yes, she's come round." Dr. Thorpe closed his bag and looked from one to another of them with quick, speculative gray eyes. "But you won't be able to question her any more tonight."

The slight antagonism in his voice was human enough, in the circumstances, but George's ear was becoming acutely tuned to every inflection that concerned Annet. Thirty-five, not bad-looking, in professional attendance on her for five years or so—on those rare occasions, at least, when she needed attention: yes, this might very well be another of her many mute, unnoticed victims.

"I wasn't thinking of trying. Is she going to be all right?"

"Physically there's not much the matter with her. It was a long faint, but she came out of it fairly well in the end. She seems to be in a state of deep and genuine shock, but physically she's as strong as a horse, there'll be no ill effects. Just leave her alone for tonight, that's all."

"Will you come in and see her tomorrow morning? I'd like to have your all-clear before I talk to her again, and I'll go very gently. But it's urgent that it should be as soon as possible."

"Very well," said the doctor with tightening lips, "I'll look in and see her before surgery. Call me about nine, and I'll give you my report."

"When she's slept on it, she may be willing to talk to me freely. I think you must see it's the best, the only thing she can do to help herself now. If you have any influence with her, try to get her to realize it." He included all of them in that request, and saw the doctor's tight, reserved face ease a little. "I've got a job to do, but it isn't to hurt Annet. A part of it is to save whatever can be saved for her."

"I'll bear it in mind," said the doctor.

"Do one thing more for me, will you? With your permission, Mr. Beck, I want to put a constable on guard here in your grounds. I'd be obliged, doctor, if you'd stay here with Annet until he arrives."

They stared eye to eye for a second, then the doctor said quietly, "Very well, I'll go back to her."

Beck turned and shuffled his way to the stairs after him, a wretched, wilted figure, babbling feeble daily platitudes, trying to pretend there was a grain of normality left in his life, where there was nothing but a waste of wreckage like a battlefield.

"I'll be off now," said George, glad, if anything, to be left confronting Mrs. Beck, with whom, it was clear, he would have to deal if he wanted to get sense out of anyone. "I shall have to take this ring with me, you understand that?"

"Yes, I understand." She looked down pallidly at the thin, bright circlet. "Do you think—is it possible that they—?"

"I think it very unlikely. This is a symbol, that's all. And a promise. It isn't so easy to get married in a hurry without a fair amount of money, and you see they can't have had much between them."

She flinched at that, his sound reasons for thinking so were only too clear.

"And in the circumstances," he said gently, "I think you should hope and pray that they didn't manage it."

She whispered, "Yes!" hardly audibly.

"Don't let her go to work tomorrow, even if she wants to. I want you to keep a close guard on her, and hold her available only to us. Don't take anyone into your confidence, not yet, at any rate. Better

telephone Mrs. Blacklock in the morning, and say
Annet has a return of her cold."

"Yes," she said again, dully, "I expect that would
be best."

"And I need, if you have one, a good recent picture
of her."

Photographs of Annet were so few in the house,
now Tom came to think of it, that their rarity shed
light on her absence of vanity. When had he even
seen her peering at her makeup in a mirror with the
devoted attention of most girls? Mrs. Beck brought a
postcard portrait, the latest she had, and George
pocketed it after one thoughtful glance again at the
lovely, troubling face.

"Thank you. You shall have it back, I promise
you." Would she get the original back as surely? He
wished he knew the answer to that. "I'll leave you in
peace now. And believe me, I'm sorry!"

"I'll see you out," said Tom, and followed him from
the room and out through the dim hall, into the
moist, mild night. The front door closed almost
stealthily upon the tragedy within.

"It can't be true!" said Tom, suddenly in total
revolt. The rupture was too brutal and extreme
between this immemorial border stability, the continuity that made nothing of wars and centuries and
dissensions, and that abrupt and strident descent
into the cheapest and shallowest of ephemeral
crimes. A mean little incident, a quick raid and a
random blow, merely for money, for the means to buy
things for Annet, to take Annet about in style—
everything Annet didn't want. The offense against
her, the debasing of her immoderate love, almost as
capital a crime as the killing of the old man. She
couldn't have known. It was the death of everything

she had wanted from love. No, she couldn't possibly have known.

"It can," said George grimly. "It happens all the time."

Did he mean merely this sordid, characteristic latter-day killing for profit, or the unbelievable misunderstanding and profanation of love implied in it? There was no knowing; he was so much deeper than he seemed, you only saw the abyss when you were already falling.

"We think we have sound relationships," said George, answering the doubt beyond doubt, "and suddenly there's a word said or a thing done, so shatteringly out of key that you find yourself alone, and know you've never actually touched your partner at any point, or said a word in the same language. And it doesn't always even absolve you from loving, when it happens. That's the hell of it."

"There's nothing I can do," said Tom, "except tell you everything I know. There's only one thing you haven't heard already. They don't know about it, I never told them, but I went over the Hallowmount yesterday morning, early, to see if there were any signs of a vehicle having been up there recently. I found tracks of a motorbike or a scooter, there's no telling which." He described them, and traced them again to the first gate. "It seemed to me that someone must have brought her back that way, the night before. After the showers this afternoon the grass and moss will have sprung back and smoothed them out, most likely, but there may be a trace left here and there. And I can show you exactly where they were."

"Then you shall, early tomorrow. If you wouldn't mind turning out about seven? The track up from the south—Abbot's Bale and beyond. Yes, I see that," said George, musing darkly under the hollies by the gate. "But why the same route back? She left in broad daylight, without luggage, in her everyday clothes, and that improbable way. All very understandable. But in the dark he could surely have come round and dropped her quietly at the corner of the lane."

"But not without using up quite a bit more time over his return, because he'd have had to come right round the hill, one end or the other. And maybe it was urgent that he should get home. He may have watchful parents, too," said Tom with a hollow smile.

"Probably has! They often turn out to belong to the most respectable citizens around," reflected George wryly, "and they're always at a loss to understand what they've done to deserve it."

"But Annet—" He looked up briefly and bitterly at the lighted window; no shadows moved across the pale curtains. "Do you have to put a police guard on her? Where could she run to, even if she tried to get out?"

"I wasn't thinking so much of Annet running," said George in a deceptively mild and deprecating voice. He caught the wondering glance that questioned his purpose, and said more abruptly, with no expression at all, "Hasn't it dawned on you yet that this lover of hers has killed once already? And that only Annet knows who he is?"

He walked away into the dark. Shaken to the heart, Tom protested softly and wildly after him, "He wouldn't hurt *her*? Damn it, he *loves* her!"

"He did," came wafting back to him hollowly as the car door slammed. "Before he was frightened for himself."

* * *

Mrs. Beck was nowhere to be seen when Tom went back into the house; and Beck was sitting slumped in a chair, clutching a glass that shook in his hands and slopped shivering waves of whiskey and soda onto his trousers. When he lifted it to his mouth it chattered against his false teeth; when he propped it steadyingly against his body it chattered against his waistcoat buttons. His glasses sagged sidelong down his nose, exposing one moist, hopeless eye, while the other was still seen monstrously magnified behind the lens. He must have downed one drink already, and spilled half of it. And he hadn't forgotten to get out a second glass. Tom's heart sank at sight of it, though he needed at least one shot, perhaps, to steady him. If this was going to be the way of escape, he wanted no part of it; he needed all his wits, he had thinking to do. And yet how could he go away and leave this wretched wreck to sweat and shiver alone? He wasn't fit to be left.

"He's gone, is he? Come and have a drink, Kenyon. I don't usually indulge, but I felt I needed something to steady my nerves." He cast a hunted look toward the ceiling. "My wife's with Annet. I don't know! You don't think it could be all a mistake?" he pleaded pathetically, and shrank from the direct encounter of their eyes. "No, I suppose not. If the man's dead— But it's some mistake about Annet. She couldn't have picked up that sort of young man. Bad as it is with her, I'm sure that can't be true. She wouldn't encourage the wrong type of boy. She's hard to please, our Annet. She never liked the flashy type. These teddy boys, they used to ask her to dance, and she'd dance with them, and be polite, but they never got anywhere with her. Myra always tells us what kind of evening they have."

Myra always tells us! Not Annet. And Annet knew, none better, that Myra always told them, that her very function was always to tell them. The closer you watch, thought Tom, the more you do not see. You didn't trust her—I wonder why, in the first place? There must have been a time when she was to be trusted absolutely—you didn't trust her, and you wouldn't let her have her soul to herself, but she got it in spite of you, and shut you out from it. And it's late now to complain of what she did with it, unaided and unadvised.

"But you haven't got a drink, my dear boy; do help yourself to a drink. I'm sure you need—we all need a little reinforcement. Please! Let me!"

He struggled to rise and reach the bottle, and there was nothing to be done but forestall him. Tom made his glass pale with soda, and hid its insipid color with a careful hand.

"And then, in Birmingham, is that feasible! I ask you! No, no, there's some mistake, it was another girl. How could Annet know a young man in Birmingham? She's hardly ever been there even overnight, only once or twice with Mrs. Blacklock to educational conferences or extramural classes, you know. And now and then shopping, of course, with her mother, or with Myra, but only for the day. It's absurd! With so little opportunity, how could she possibly have formed an intimate association with a young fellow in the city? It's a mistake, isn't it? It must be a mistake."

"If it is," said Tom encouragingly, though encouraging was the last thing he felt just then, "the police will find it out. You can be sure of that. The best possible thing Annet can do is tell George Felse everything she did during the weekend. There'll be

people who've seen her, and can confirm her story, if
only she'll speak."

"Yes—yes, that's true, isn't it? There are always
ways of verifying such statements. If only she'll tell
us! And even here at home, you know, Tom, where
does she ever go alone for more than an hour or two?
Myra's always with her when she goes to dances,
and we see to it that they have reliable escorts. And
even if she works late the Blacklocks always send
her home by car. From choir practice Mr. Collins
walks her home, or Mr. Blacklock brings her himself. It isn't as if we've been neglectful. All our
friends think the world of her, and care for her like
their own. When *can* she have formed an undesirable
acquaintance? We should have known. Someone
would have warned us."

Only too surely they would. That was why she had
to learn to cover every trace, to erase the very prints
of her feet where she had passed, to open her own
escape hatches into the underworld below the Hallowmount.

"There was the affair of young Miles, of course.
But that was understandable folly. And since then
we've watched her even more carefully."

What was the sense in telling him now that that
was where they'd made their mistake? And in fact it
was only one in a wilderness of mistakes, and not,
Tom felt, the fatal one. Something else had gone
wrong with Annet's daughterhood, something basic
and incurable.

"Don't upset yourself, that won't help. You've always done your best for her, everybody knows that."
He leaned and extracted the quivering glass from
Beck's fingers, for it was slipping slowly through
them as he watched. Beck did not seem to notice its
going, only in a distant way to be relieved to find his

hands free. He took his quaking head between them, staring blindly through a mist half drunkenness and half tears.

"We did do our best. They'll find out they've made a mistake. It wasn't Annet. It couldn't have been."

But he was crying his denials because he knew it had been. Her charged stillness, braced to bear whatever pressures were loosed on her, and still cover up her known sins for the sake of her partner; this spoke loudly enough. And her cry of passionate denial and fearful realization when she was forced to contemplate the sin of which she had not known; and the violence of her retreat into a semblance of death; and the ring on its ribbon round her neck.

The old man was weeping feebly, without even knowing it, letting the tears find a desultory way down the furrows of his gray, despairing face.

"It wasn't good enough, that's all, our best wasn't good enough. Where did we go wrong? Was it my fault? I never carried much weight, you know, not with anyone. Managing the children at school was too much for me sometimes. They always know," he said drearily, "who can hold his own with them, and who can't. I never could find out how it was done. But to fail with Annet! To fall short even with her!"

"Nonsense, of course you haven't always fallen short. You mustn't think like that, what good does it do? The best girl in the world can very well throw away her affection on a bad lot, we all know it happens. Is that your fault?"

Tom's voice was gentle and reasonable; he marveled at it himself, while his mind dallied with the thought of filling the old man to the brim with whiskey, and sinking him completely. Then at least he could be manhandled to bed, and he'd be blessedly silent, affording a respite for himself and everyone else. But he'd probably be sick, and not even put himself happily to sleep. No, better not risk it. Let him talk. If it helped him, at least somebody was getting something out of it.

Drearily, drearily the fumbling voice, thickening a little now, proceeded lead-footed along its inevitable downhill road of confession, laying out his inadequacies like pilgrim stones along the way.

"But then, why should I be expected to succeed with her? You don't know, Tom, do you—about Annet? I've never told you. We never told anyone. It isn't the sort of thing you write to your friends—"

He was laughing now, and still crying. Maybe the whiskey was taking hold, and he'd pass out. Tom put a hand on his arm and shook him gently.

"That's all right, there's nothing you need to tell me. Wait till tomorrow. There'll be new developments then, maybe they'll have found the real girl they're looking for."

"They have found her," said Beck with dreadful clarity, and gripped Tom's arm in his heavy, trembling hands. "I want to tell you. It's been on my mind so long, I've got to tell someone. She isn't mine, you see. Things might have been different if she had been. I never understood her, I never had any influence over her. I was always ashamed and afraid, because she isn't even mine."

He sagged into Tom's shoulder and lay there, as it seemed, thankfully, almost comfortably. And my God, what do you say now? What can you say?

"You're a little tight, you know, better come to bed and rest. You don't mean this. All parents have these doubts sooner or later, it's one of the hazards of fatherhood."

His own voice sounded to him like the phony effort of one privately in acute pain. He got to his feet brusquely, wild to break up this inconceivable party, and lugged Beck up after him, propping him against the arm of the chair until he could get a firm hold on him. And Beck yielded. When had anyone pulled or pushed or propelled him, that he had not yielded? But he went on talking, too, with remorseless misery, all across the room and all along the empty hall.

"You don't believe me. But it's true. *My wife told me,*" he said with self-mutilating satisfaction. "She'd waited long enough for me to give her a child. In the end she got one where she could. She never told me who. She said what was that to me? I couldn't help her. She held it against me. She still does."

Somehow, he was never very clear how, Tom got him up the stairs and into his bedroom, and there frankly abandoned him. Sick with disgust and pity, he shut himself into the bathroom and washed the sweat and the prickling of shame from his face in cold water. He felt like vomiting, but he hadn't had enough whiskey. Maybe he ought to go down again and put himself out for the count. It would be one way of shutting the door on all this for a little while.

Was it true? Had she ever really told him such a thing? She might have, she was a woman who could if driven to it, and he was a man to whom it could be done, so crushable that in the end there might be nothing to be done with him but crush him once for all, and finish it. But even if she had told him that, need it necessarily be true? Or a gesture of hatred and cruelty engendered by the bitter frustration of their marriage?

Tom went over and over the bleak sentences he had tried hard not to hear and could not now forget, and for the life of him he couldn't judge what was truth and what wasn't.

But Annet herself was the heart of the evidence.

Was there anything of Beck there, in her clear-cut, self-contained, fastidious dignity? And if she was alien, and the root of their alienation, she might well be wandering, lost, trying to find her own way in a desert without asking for help from anyone. And if she knew—? How could she know? No one could be so inhuman, so insanely self-centered as to tell her? But *if* she knew—

And there was nothing he could do for her. Nothing to help or comfort her. Nothing, nothing to make her aware of him.

CHAPTER 6

They came down from the Hallowmount in the fresh morning light, and separated on the road below, Tom heading for school, George for the southern end of the ridge and the straggling village of Abbot's Bale in the long, bare cleft of Middlehope.

There was an hour yet before he could call the doctor and receive his verdict on Annet; and when he went to Fairford this time he must have a sergeant and a constable with him. Meantime, he could view the escape route and its strategic possibilities, the filling stations, the natives, the chances of picking up evidence. Annet was striking in any circumstances; even flying past on the pillion of a motorbike (probably stripped of its silencer and ridden with vile technique and viler manners), she might be noticed. If they'd halted at a filling station with healthily normal young men in the forecourt instead of girls, she certainly would be. Someone might remember.

"So Miss Myra Gibbons always reports back, does

she?" said George skeptically. He had received a half-account of last night's unsought confidences, but it stopped well short of the revelation about Annet's parentage. If anyone retold that tale, short of the most desperate emergency, it would have to be Beck himself.

"Not as fully as father supposes, I fancy. I bet I know one or two things that never got back to the parents. As, for instance, that a couple of uniformed men had to show up at the hall late one Saturday night, to stop what promised to be a first-class fight. Over Annet. Not her fault, unless she's to blame for looking like she does. A handful of the local ton-up club had taken to looking in at the ballroom about ten to ten, just in time to beat the no entry or reentry after ten rule. They know a good-looker when they see one, and they think a good-looker ought to go for their kind. Annet didn't do anything except dance with the leader of the bunch when he asked her. It was her escort who objected when he promptly asked her again. There've been other clashes too, occasionally, less serious. Oh, yes, even among the respectable and ultra-respectable, Annet can set the sparks flying."

"Then this youngster who tried to corner her had a motorbike," said Tom hopefully. "All the round-the-houses brigade seem to have big, powerful jobs, five hundreds mostly. What beats me is they never seem to do anything or go anywhere with them—only round and round the block."

"Oh, they do now. They go all the three-quarters of a mile between their favorite roosting ground on the corner of the square and the Rainbow Café on the edge of town. And back. One or two," admitted George on reflection, "might have the enterprise to get as far as Birmingham. One or two, literally, might get a good deal farther and venture a good deal more, but I wouldn't put it higher than two. And one of 'em's the youngster who fancied her at the dance. And he works," said George reflectively, sliding into the driving seat of his almost-new M.G., "at a haulage concern in Abbot's Bale."

"He does?" A spark of hope kindled professionally in Tom's eye at the thought that the hunt might veer so blessedly away from the school. Not one of ours! One of the black-leather lads, born scapegoats! But could so close an association be formed over a few dances, without a single strictly private meeting? Maybe it could, but the odds seemed against it. He'd never, for instance, taken her home afterwards. She always went home with Myra. Or did her parents merely suppose that she did?

"Of course," he said dubiously, "it seems more likely, on the whole, that it was someone from Birmingham, someone who came here to fetch her, and isn't necessarily known here."

"With Annet planning the operation and telling him exactly where to wait for her and how to get there? It could well be." It could; she had the stuff of command in her, and passion enough for two if the partner proved deficient. "We're checking at both ends, anyhow," said George. "Properly speaking it's Birmingham's case, not ours."

He was turning the key in the ignition when Tom came loping across to ask, "You didn't ask your boy, did you? About my questioning them both?"

He was glad to have the full story of that incident off his chest, but very reluctant indeed that it should get back to Dominic. Nothing had been published yet about Annet. Nothing would, if they could get the information they urgently needed some other way; and surely, surely she'd talk this morning, and

save herself? It would be superhuman to keep silence still. Supposing she told everything, did her
best to cooperate, and she herself turned out to have
known nothing about the crime, then her part in
the affair, even if it could not be suppressed, would
be forever toned down to its most innocent, and
maybe need never erupt into the headlines at all.

"I asked him about their weekend. He told me
what he told you." George's eyes did not commit him
at all as to how completely he had believed; but the
ghost of a rather rueful smile showed for a moment.
"I didn't say I had any deep motives for asking, and
I didn't say you'd tipped me off—even inadvertently.
But I suspect he already smells a sizeable rat."

"Did he say anything to make you think so?"

George's smile lost its sourness for an instant.
What Dominic had actually said, and very belliger-
ently, was, "What business is it of Brash 'Arry's,
anyhow?" But there was no need to broadcast that.
"My thumbs pricked, that's all." This time he did
turn the key. "So long, Tom, and thanks!"

He drove southward along the flank of the Hallowmount, past the turning to Wastfield, past the new
plantations, on toward the slow, descending tail of
the ridge, that took such an unconscionable time to
decline far enough to permit the passage of a road.
Yes, if the boy had needed to keep a strict timetable
on his return home he might very well be forced to
cut out that long drive round, and drop Annet where
he had picked her up, to climb back over the hill.
But why not simply drop her on the bus route to the
village, and let her ride the last stage home as
though she'd been to a cinema? Who would have
thought anything about her appearance on an
evening bus? It might even have disarmed some who
had been gleefully scenting a trail of fresh trouble.

But half the "why's" involved in any crime must be answered without too nice a reference to logic. At our best we are not creatures of absolute reason and consistency. Having killed, we are not at our best.

Not much time to do more than run into Abbot's Bale, and take a quick look at the upland road which soon dwindled into a cart track, plunging at last through a farm gate to climb the first rough pasture; and then fill up at Hopton's as an excuse for a word with old man Hopton, who was sure to be the only one pottering about the forecourt at this hour. A powerful, bowed, cross-grained little elderly man with an obstinate, surly face that never took anyone in for long. It was one of the very few places where George and the probation officer had even been able to place their most perilous problem boys with good will and confidence. If they failed there, you were on your way to despairing of them. Some did fail; there were more than enough to despair about in human nature, twentieth-century style. Some, against all the odds, stuck it out and got a stout foothold on life again; there was plenty of ground for hope, too.

George asked after the latest of them, as Hopton flicked his leather squeaking across the windscreen. Hopton opined that the latest was an idle, cheeky layabout with a chip on his shoulder as big as a Yule log; he reckoned he'd shape up about average. Rightly interpreting this as a considerably more encouraging report than it sounded, George turned to the matter that was nearer his heart.

"Ever see young Geoff Westcott these days? He's still driving for Lowthers, isn't he?"

"Hear him more than I see him. Comes clattering in to fill up sometimes, weekends. Oh, ay, he's still there. Good driver, too, on a lorry. Pity he leaves his

manners in the cab when he knocks off. He's hell on
that three-fifty of his."

"Fill up last weekend?" asked George.

"Didn't see him. Why? You got something on him?"
The shrewd old eyes narrowed on George's face
expectantly. "Didn't see him since Thursday, come
to think of it."

"He's clean, as far as I know," said George amiably. "When on Thursday? Just a little job involving a
motorbike, nothing special on him, just eliminating
the barely possibles."

"He was in in the middle of the afternoon. I
remember young Sid asked him what he was doing
romping around in working hours, and he said he
had three extra days saved up from the summer
holidays, and was taking 'em before the weather
broke altogether."

George digested this with a prickle of satisfaction
stirring his scalp. He fished out from his wallet one
of the barely dry copies the police photographer had
made him from Annet's photograph.

"What poor girl's he standing up for what other
poor girl, these days?"

"Mate," said Hopton, very dryly indeed, "you got it
wrong. These days the girls ain't surplus round here
like they used to be. It's the men who get stood up,
even the ones with three-fifties. And if they don't
like it, they know what they can do. They're relieved
if they can get a girl to go steady, they lay off the
tricks unless they want to be left high and dry."

"You're not telling me young Geoff's got a steady?"

"Hasn't he, though! Wouldn't dare call Martha
Blount anything but steady, would you?"

"No," owned George freely, "I wouldn't!" If Martha
Blount meant marriage, the odds were that she
wasn't wasting her time. There were still Blounts

round the Hallowmount nearly three centuries after Tabby blundered in and out of fairyland. "How long's this been going on?"

"Few weeks now, but it's got a permanent look about it."

"Ever seen him with this one? Before or since." George showed the grave and daunting face, the straight, wide eyes that made it seem a desecration to mention her in such light and current terms.

"Oh, I know *her*. That's the old schoolmaster's girl, from up the other valley. Used to teach my nephew, he did, they nearly drove him up the wall before he got out of it and moved to Fairford. She's a beauty, that one," he said fondly, tilting his head appreciatively over Annet's picture. "No, I've never seen *her* with Geoff Westcott. Wouldn't expect to, neither."

No, and of course they'd know that, whether they ever acknowledged it or not, and take care not to affront the village's notions of what was to be accepted as normal and what was not. Still, one asked.

"Now if you'd said *him*," said Hopton unexpectedly, and nodded across the street.

Outside the single hardware shop a young man in a leather jacket of working rather than display cut had just propped a heavy motorcycle at the pavement's edge, and was striding toward the shop doorway. A tall, dark young man, perhaps twenty-five, scarcely older, possibly younger; uncovered brown hair very neatly trimmed, a vigorous, confident walk, none of the signs of convulsed adolescence left about him. And a striking face, dark and reticent as a gypsy, with a proud, curled, sensitive mouth. He was in the shop only a minute, evidently collecting something which had been ordered and was ready for him, tools of some kind; a gleam of color and of steel as he stowed the half-swathed bundle in his saddlebag, straddled the machine with a long, leisurely movement of his whole body from head to toes, kicked it into life, and roared away from the pavement and along the single street. In a few moments he was out of sight.

"Seen her with *him* times enough," said Hopton, as if that was perfectly to be expected.

"Have you, indeed! And who is he? I don't even know him."

"Name of Stockwood. He's another of 'em. See him behind the wheel of the Bentley, and butter wouldn't melt in his mouth. Put him astride one of them there B.S.A.s they keep for running up and down to the plantations and the farms, and he sprouts horns. He does look after them, though, I will say that. They come in now and again to be serviced—some rough rides they get, the estate being what it is—and you can tell a machine that's cared for."

"Are you telling me," asked George intently, light dawning, "that that's Mrs. Blacklock's chauffeur? Since when? There used to be a thin, gray-haired fellow named Braidie."

"Retired about three months ago, and this chap came. Name of Stockwood. I've seen *him* driving the Beck lass home often enough."

George stood looking thoughtfully after the faint plume of dust that lingered where the rider had vanished. So that was the reliable human machine that guarded Annet from undesirable encounters by regularly driving her home. Pure luck that he should be seen for the first time not with the car, but with one of the estate utilities, and consequently out of strict uniform. Chauffeurs are anonymous, automatic, invisible; but there went a live, feeling and very personable young man. Was it quite impossible that Annet, startled and disarmed by the change from Braidie's elderly, familiar person, should steal glances along her shoulder in the Bentley, on all those journeys home, and see the man instead of the chauffeur?

"All right," said George, "break off. No use going on like this, leave me alone with her."

He got up from his chair and went to the window of the living room, and stood staring out vaguely through a mist, as though he had been wearing glasses and steamed them opaque with the heat of his own exhaustion. Sweat ran, slowly and heavily, between his shoulder blades. Who would have thought she had the strength in her to resist and resist and resist, fending off solicitude as implacably as reproaches? She looked so fragile that you'd have thought she could be broken in the hands; and it seemed she was indestructible and immovable.

He heard them get up obediently and leave the room, Price first with his notebook, that had nothing in it but a record of unanswered questions, then Sergeant Grocott, lightfooted, closing the door gently behind him. Mrs. Beck had not moved from the chair by the couch.

"Alone," said George.

"I have a right to be present. Annet is my daughter. If she wants me—"

"Ask her," he said without turning his head, "if she wants you."

"It's all right, Mother," said Annet, breaking her silence for the third time in two hours. Once she had said, "Good morning!" and once, "I'm sorry!" but after that nothing more. "Please!" she said now. "Mr. Felse has a right. And I don't mind."

The chair shrieked offense on the polished floor. Mrs. Beck withdrew; the door closed again with a frigid click, and George and Annet were alone in the room.

He went back to her, and drew a chair close to the studio couch on which she was ensconced in the protective ceremony of convalescence. Mrs. Beck, surely, had arranged the tableau, to disarm, to afflict him with a sense of guilt and inhibit him from hectoring her daughter. He doubted if Annet had even noticed. Silent, pale and withdrawn, the small painful frown fixed on her brow as though she agonized without respite at a problem no one else could help her to solve, she looked full at him while she denied him, as though she saw him from an infinite distance but with particular clarity. Bereft even of her fantasy wedding ring, she clung at least to her silence, an absolute silence now.

"Annet, listen to me. We know you were there. We've got a firm identification of you from two witnesses now. And your ring came from the dead man's stock. All this is fact. Established. Nobody's going to shake it now. We know there was a man with you. We know you waited for him on the corner. We know the exact time, and it fits in with the medical estimate of the time the old man died. This is murder. An inoffensive old man, who'd never done anything to you, who didn't even know you. Who'd never seen his murderer before. Just a chance victim, because the time was right and the street was empty, and there was money just being checked up in the till. A quick profit, and what's a life or so in the cause? That's not you, Annet. I know society is dull and censorious and often wrong, I know its values aren't always the highest. But if you diverge from its standards, it surely isn't going to be for lower ones. There's only one thing you can do now, and only one side on which you can range yourself. Tell me what happened. Tell me the whole story."

She shook her head, very slightly, her eyes wide and steady upon his face. She let him take her hands and hold them, tightly and warmly; her fingers even seemed to accept his clasp with more than a passive consent. But she said nothing.

"Have I to tell it to you? I believe I can, and not be far out. You were coming past the shop together, maybe the old man was just putting the mesh gate across, ready to close. Your companion stopped suddenly, and told you to wait for him. Probably you were surprised, probably you wanted to go with him, but he wouldn't let you. He stood you on the corner, well out of earshot of what he intended to do, and told you he was going to buy you something, and it was to be a surprise. And you did what he wanted, because you wanted nothing else in the world but to do everything he wanted, because all your will was never to deny him anything. And maybe what he intended, then, was only robbery if he hadn't hit too hard. Frightened boys turning violent for the first time frequently do."

The hands imprisoned in his suddenly plunged and struggled in their confinement for an instant. Her face shook, and was still again.

"I know," said George, sick with pity. "I told you, none of this goes with you, nothing except your loving him. That happens, who can blame you for that? Personally, I don't think you knew a thing about either robbery or murder until I sprang it on you last night. He came back to you and gave you the ring, and so much of you was concentrated on that—as a gift and a promise, as a kind of private sacrament—that if he was agitated or uneasy you didn't notice it. He hurried you away, and all you knew was that he'd bought you a wedding ring, on impulse, on a sentimental impulse at that, with money he couldn't really afford. A sweet, silly thing to do. But he left Jacob Worrall dead or dying in the back room, switched off the shop lights and drew the gate to across the doorway. And nobody saw him. Nobody knows who he is. Nobody but you, Annet."

He had got so far when he saw that she was crying, with the extraordinary tranquility of despair, her face motionless, the tears gathering heavily in her dilated eyes, and overflowing slowly down her cheeks. No convulsive struggle with her grief, she sat still and let it possess her, aware of the uselessness of all movement and all sound.

"Surely you see that the best thing you can do, ultimately, even for him, is tell me the whole story. Who is he, this young man of yours? Oh, he loved you very much—I know! He wanted to be with you, to give you things, because he loved you. He wanted more than a stolen weekend, he wanted to take you away with him for good. But he had to have money to make that possible. A lot of money. And he took what he thought was a chance, when it offered. But think what his state must be now, Annet! Do you think it's enviable to be a murderer? Even the kind that gets away with it? Think about it, Annet!"

And maybe she did think about it; she sat gazing at him great-eyed, perhaps unaware of the tears that coursed slowly down her face, but she never spoke. She listened, she understood, there was a communication, of that he had no doubt; but it was still one-sided. He could not make her speak.

"If you love him," said George, very gently and simply, "and I think you do, you'll want to do the best for him, and save him from the worst. And being convicted, even dying, isn't necessarily the worst, you know."

The word passed into her with a sharp little jerk and quiver, like a poisoned dart, but it did not startle her.

"You see, I'm not lying to you. This is capital murder, and we both know it. It may not come to that extremity; but it could. But even so, Annet, if it were me, I'd rather pay than run. You can't save him now from killing, but you can spare him the remembering and hiding and running, the lying down with his dead man every night, and getting up with him every morning—"

Still she kept her silence, all she had left; but she bowed forward suddenly out of her tranced grief, felt toward George's shoulder with nuzzling cheek and brow, and let herself lie against him limp and weary, her closed eyelids hidden on his breast. He gathered both her hands into one of his, slipped the other arm round her gently, and held her as long as she cared to rest so. He made no use of the contact to persuade or move her; the compassion and respect he felt for her put it clean out of his power.

She drew away from him at last with a sigh that was dragged up from the roots of her body. She looked up, while his face was still out of focus to her, and in a soft, urgent voice she said, "Let me go! Don't watch me! Take your man away from the house, and let me go."

"Annet, I can't."

"Please! Please! Take him away and leave me free. Tell them not to watch me. You could if you would."

"No," said George heavily, "it's impossible."

She took her hands from him slowly, and turned her face away, and the silence was back upon her like an invisible armor through which he could not penetrate. He got up slowly, and stood looking down at her with a shadowed face.

"You realize, Annet, that if you won't give us the information we need, we must get it elsewhere. So far we've kept you from the press, but if you won't help us we shall have to make use of your name and photograph. There'll be people who'll remember having seen you during the weekend. There must be someone who knows where you spent those nights in Birmingham. Time is very important, and you can't be spared beyond today. You understand that?"

She nodded. The averted face shivered once, but she made no protest.

"I ask you again to make that unnecessary. Tell me, and we shan't have to put you in the pillory."

"No," said Annet absolutely; and a moment later, in indifferent reassurance, "It doesn't matter."

He understood that she was disclaiming any consideration for herself, and acknowledging his right and duty to expend her if he must. More, after her fashion she was comforting him.

He turned his back on her wearily, and went out without a word more. He could get tears from her, he could get warmth from her, but he could not get words. What was the use of persisting in this impossible siege? But he knew he'd be back before the day was out. How could he leave her to destroy herself?

"I'm leaving a man on guard," he said to Beck in the hall. "And I want you to let me place a policewoman in the house with Annet, as an additional precaution. It's for her protection, you surely realize that. Make sure that somebody's always with her, don't let her out of your sight. And don't let anyone in to her but the police."

He wasn't going to lose Annet if he could help it, however wantonly she was offering herself as a

sacrificial victim. Let me go, indeed! George
shrugged his way morosely into his coat, and went to
report total failure to the Chief of the County C.I.D.

"Do you want her arrested, or don't you?" demanded
Detective-Superintendent Duckett, before the tale
was finished. "Seems to me you don't know your own
mind. If she was my girl, I'd hustle her behind bars
and heave a sigh of relief. And I'd make sure of
putting her out of reach before the evening paper
rolls out on the streets at one o'clock. We've done it
now."

"Had to," said George glumly. "There's nothing to
be got out of her, and we can't afford to lose today. I
warned her. She knows the odds. Not that that lets
us out."

"Well, if you've put the brightest girl we've got in
the house with her, and left Lockyer on guard
outside, I don't see what harm she can come to."

All the same, they had crossed a Rubicon there
was no recrossing and they knew it. Once the
regional *Evening News* hit the streets all the world
would know that Annet Beck was "expected to be
able to help the police" in their enquiries into the
Bloome Street murder; that she had been identified
by witnesses as having been in the district at the
time; and that further witnesses to her movements
in Birmingham were being sought, with a photograph of Annet to remind them in case they were in
doubt of the face that went with the name.

"No," said George. "I don't want to arrest her. I
admit I was tempted to do it the easy way, and put
her clean out of his reach. He may not have much
faith in her silence; and however surely he committed the crime for her—in a sense—in the first place,
his terror now is liable to be all for himself, and

all-consuming. He must have been wildly uneasy already; he'll be frightened to death when he sees the paper. But there it is—I don't want to bring her in, because I'm convinced she's absolutely innocent—apart from this damned mistaken loyalty of hers after the event."

"Well, let's hope the photograph will bring in somebody who saw and remembers them in Birmingham. Somebody who can give us a good description of the boy. Up to now, what do we really know about him? No one's admitted to seeing him, he left no distinguishable prints on the glass cases or the latch of the door or the candlestick—soft leather gloves, apparently. Trouble is, they all know the ropes by now. He's still totally invisible and anonymous, to everybody but the Beck girl. He may be from anywhere, he may be anyone. All we can say with reasonable certainty is that he must be someone young enough and attractive enough to engage a girl's attention. And what does that mean? Most of the young ones you see about, these days, you wouldn't expect a smart girl to want to be seen dead with, but they break their hearts over 'em just the same. And what else do we know about him? That he's got no money. He has to get it the quick, modern way in order to be able to take his girl about in style. But which of 'em have got money? They make what most of us used to keep a family on, but they're always broke before the end of the week. And that's it. A blank."

"Except that he *may* have a motorbike," said George, and stuffed his notes somberly back into his pocket. "*If* we accept that the tracks down in Middlehope are relevant. Nothing positive from London yet on our friend's weekend?"

"Nothing conclusive. He was home, that's true

enough, but in and out a good deal, apparently. I asked them to fill in Saturday evening, and let the rest go. From London to Birmingham is an evening out these days. Coaches do it in no time, up the M1. I called them again half an hour ago, but they won't be rushed. I hoped we'd get that, at least, before we had to issue the handout, but it makes no difference. We'd have had to publish, the grapevine was getting in first. So how does it stand from the other end now? How's your list of possibles?"

"Wide open. Her parents think they had a boy-proof fence erected round her, but you and I know there's no such thing. There were three or four rather dull and respectable lads they allowed to squire her to dances, but always with the Gibbons girl in tow. But who knows whether they stay dull and respectable once they're out of sight of the older generation? Here are the names of the approved, and we're checking up on them, but I'm not expecting much from them. Still, you never know. Then there's young Geoff Westcott, who would certainly *not* have been approved by mother. He's danced with Annet several times, and started a fight over her at least once. And he chose to take the few days' holiday Lowthers owed him from the summer this last week-end, and filled up at old man Hopton's on Thursday afternoon. Scott is nosing around to find out what he did with his time. And then there's an interesting outsider. I saw him this morning in Abbot's Bale. Mrs. Beck always reassured herself that the Black-locks took care to send Annet home in the car when she worked late, or whenever the nights dropped dark early, or there was bad weather. If Regina or hubby didn't drive her home, they sent her with the chauffeur. All very nice and safe, and when could she possibly have struck up an undesirable acquain-

tance? But was it so nice and safe? Braidie was
sixty-five and past caring, but Braidie, it seems,
retired about three months ago. The fellow they've
got now—I wonder if the Becks have even
noticed?—is one Stockwood, twenty-fourish, good-
looking and altogether presentable. And because
Mrs. Blacklock was away at her conference, and
Blacklock prefers to drive himself, Stockwood was
given the weekend off after he'd driven Mrs. Blacklock down to Gloucester, and he reported back only
to fetch her home on Wednesday. Annet had the
opportunity to get to know *him*, all right. Probably
three, four times a week he's had her in the car alone
with him."

"And that's all?"

George said, with his eyes fixed on the roofs of Hill
Street outside the window, and the small crease of
personal anxiety between his brows, "It wouldn't do
any harm to get on to Capel Curig, and ask them to
check up on the boys and their campsite, I suppose.
Shouldn't take them long, we can tell them exactly
where they were supposed to be."

"I did," said Duckett smugly, and grinned at him
broadly through the smoke of his pipe and the
stubbornly unmilitary thicket of his mustache; and
anything that could raise a genuine grin that day was
more than welcome. "I should have told you
sooner—you can cross off young Mallindine. They
were there, all right, both of 'em. We found people
who saw them regularly two or three times a day,
one couple who climbed with them all day Sunday.
Saturday night around the time we're interested in,
know where they were? In the local, with a couple of
half pints. The barman remembers, because he
asked 'em, by way of a leg-pull, if they were eighteen. He says one of 'em looked down his nose at him

and said yes, and the other blushed till his ears lit up."

"Good God!" said George blankly, manfully suppressing the thankful lift of his heart. "I didn't know he could."

"Plenty of things you don't know about your Dom, you can safely bet on that. But his friend's in the clear over this, and your boy hasn't had to tell any lies for him. As for his crime against the Licensing Act, you take my tip, George, don't waste it. Save it up till the next time he gets uppish with his old man, and then flatten him with it. You'll have him walking on tiptoe for weeks, thinking you're Sherlock Holmes in person."

"I wish to God I was!" owned George, sighing, and rose somewhat wearily to put on his coat. Something was gained, at least, if Miles was safely out of the reckoning. Only let there be someone observant and reliable somewhere in Birmingham at this moment, reading the noon edition over his lunch, and suddenly arrested by Annet's recognized and remembered face. Let him be able to set another face beside it clearly, quickly, before that other turned the same page, to swallow his heart and pocket his shaking hands, and ponder at last, inescapably, that it was Annet or himself for it.

"I'm going to snatch a meal," he said, picking up his hat from Duckett's desk. "I'll be back."

He had the door open when the telephone rang. Very quietly he closed the door again, and watched Duckett palm the handset, his shaggy head on one side, his thick brows twitching.

"Ah, like that!" said Duckett, after a few minutes of silences and monosyllables, and emitted a brief and unamused snort of laughter. "Yes, thanks, it does. Clears the decks for us, anyhow, and leaves us with at least a glimmer of a lead. Yes, let us have the reports. Thanks again!" He clapped the receiver back and thrust the set away from him with a grunt that might have meant satisfaction or disgust, or a mixture of both.

"Well?" said George, his shoulder against the door.

"One more you can cross off. His parents didn't see him for most of Saturday, he came in after midnight. But there's a girl. A clinger, it seems. All Saturday afternoon and evening she never let go. You can take the story he told to you as being on the level, tiretracks and all, for what they're worth. Whoever knocked old Worrall on the head, your Number One didn't."

CHAPTER 7

The evening paper wasn't dropped into the Felse family's letter box until the last edition came in at about five o'clock. Bunty Felse was alone when it came, with the tea party, and neither husband nor son present to eat it. Dominic was always late on rugger practice afternoons, but even so he should have been home before this time. And as for George, when he was on this kind of case who could tell when she would see him?

She sat down with the paper to wait for them patiently, and Annet Beck's face looked out at her from the front page with great, mute, disconcerting eyes, beneath the query: "Have you seen this girl?"

"Anyone who remembers noticing the girl pictured above," said the beginning of the text more precisely, "with a male companion in the central or southern districts of Birmingham during last week-end, should communicate with the police."

Bunty read it through, and in fact it was as reticent as it could well be and still be exact in conveying its purpose and its urgency. She sank her head between her hands, threading her fingers into the bush of chestnut hair that was just one shade darker than Dominic's, and contemplated Annet long and thoughtfully. "A male companion," "it is believed," "helping the police in their enquiries"— such discreet, such clinical formulae, guaranteed nonactionable. But a real girl in the middle of it, and somewhere, still hidden, a real boy, maybe no older than Dominic.

They were pretty sure of their facts, that was clear. They knew when they laid hands on the partner of Annet's truancy they would have Jacob Worrall's murderer. What they didn't know, what nobody knew but Annet, was who he was. And Annet wouldn't tell. Bunty didn't have to wonder or ask how things were going for George now, she knew.

No one could identify him but Annet. And she wouldn't. Why, otherwise, should they be reduced to appealing to the public for information, and displaying Annet as bait? He might be anyone. He might be anywhere. You might go down to the grocer's on the corner and ask him for a pound of cheese, and his hands might be trembling so he could hardly control the knife. You might bump into him at a corner and put your hand on his arm to steady yourself and him as you apologized, and feel him flinch, recoiling for an instant from the dread of a more official hand on his shoulder. He might get up and give you his seat in a bus, or blare past you on a noisy motorbike at the crossing, and snarl at you to get out of his way. He might be the young clerk from the Education Department, just unfolding the paper in the bus on his way home. He'd killed a man, and he was on the run, but only one girl could give him a face or a name.

How well did he know his Annet? Do you ever know anyone well enough to stake your life on her? When all the claims of family and society and up-bringing pull the other way? If he was absolutely sure of her loyalty, there was a hope that he wouldn't try to approach her at all, that he'd just take his plunder and make a quiet getaway while he was anonymous, leaving Annet to carry the load alone. Could she love that kind of youth? Plenty of fine girls have, owned Bunty ruefully, why not Annet? It might be the best thing, because if he started running he would almost inevitably lose his nerve and run too fast, and just one slip would bring the hunt after him. Somewhere away from here, where he couldn't double back to remove, in his last despair, the one really dangerous witness.

But if he couldn't be sure of her, if he feared, as he well might, that under pressure she might break down at last and betray him, then from this moment on Annet's life was in great danger. If you're frightened to death, you stop loving, you stop thinking or feeling but in one desperate plane of reference, you fight for your life, and kill whatever threatens it. These, at least, thought Bunty, must be the reactions of an unstable young creature, not yet mature, the kind of boy who could have committed that brutal, opportunist crime in the shop in Bloome Street. The commonplace of today, the current misdemeanor, cosh the shopkeeper, clear the till, run; quick money to pay for this and future sprees, in three easy movements. It happens all the time. Preferably old men or old women in back-street shops, because they're so often solitary. No, the boy who did that wouldn't keep his love intact for long when it was his life or Annet's.

Bunty got up suddenly and went to the telephone

in the hall. It wasn't so much that she was really anxious about her offspring; just a sudden unwilling- ness to be alone with this line of thought any longer, and a feeling that company would be helpful. It might even help her to think. How could she leave alone a problem that was tormenting George?

"Eve? You haven't got Dominic there, have you?"

"I did have, sweetie, for about ten minutes, but that was half an hour ago. They blew in and went into a huddle in the corner, and then they up and made a phone call, and went off again. They brought the paper in with them. I did wonder," said Eve Mallindine, resigning the idea reluctantly, "if they'd come to you. They never said a word. And when I looked at the 'News'—well, you'll have seen it."

"Yes," said Bunty, and pondered, jutting a dubious lip. "Eve—they *were* where they said they were, surely? Over the weekend? They couldn't, either of them—"

"No," said Eve, firmly and serenely, "they couldn't. Neither of them. Not in any circumstances."

"No, of course not! My God, I must be going round the bend. It's such hell growing up, that's all. And I'm afraid to think we've got angels instead of boys— such arrogance! And there *was* the first time, for Miles—don't shoot me down in flames, but it did happen."

"Listen, honey," said Eve's bright, confident voice, for once subdued into a wholly private and unmock- ing tenderness, "it *didn't* happen. Not even that once. Don't tell anyone else. I promised Miles I wouldn't ask him anything, or tell anything, and I wouldn't now if we weren't all in a pretty sticky situation. Miles never tried to run away anywhere, with or without Annet Beck. So you can put that out of your mind."

"But they were picked up at the station," said Bunty blankly, "with two cases. And two tickets to London."

"So they were. Two cases. But both of them were Annet's."

"*Both* of them? But Bill would have *known*! For goodness' sake! He took Annet home with one case, and brought Miles back with the other. Do you mean to tell me he doesn't know the family luggage?"

Eve said, with curiosity, wonder and not a little envy, "You know, George must be a tidy-minded man, to inspire such confidence in husbands. Bill?" A brief, affectionate hoot of laughter patted his name on the head and reduced him to size. "Bill doesn't know his own shirts. Every time we dig the cases out of the attic to pack, he swears he's never seen half of them before. 'When did we buy this thing, darling?' 'I don't remember this—did we pinch it somewhere?' I could filch a tie out of his drawer and give it him for his birthday, and he wouldn't know."

"But how, then? I mean—"

"I don't know, I never asked. When Bill dropped on them and jumped to conclusions, Miles arranged it that way, that's all. And she let him. *I* got the case back to Annet afterward. I took advantage of Regina Blacklock's car to do it, but she never knew, and you knew Braidie, he was so correct he was stone-deaf to everything but what he was supposed to hear. It was very easy, I just telephoned to Annet at the hall, and asked her to get Braidie to call here when he took her home, someday when her parents would be out. So I know what I'm talking about, my love. I'd thought the poor lamb had bought it specially for the jaunt, you see, and I started to unpack it, out of pure kindness of heart and helpfulness. Thank God Bill wasn't there! All Annet's best frocks! You should

have seen his face! After he'd covered up for her so
nobly, and then to have me meddling. I tell you, I
had the honor of all mothers in my hands."

"I'll be cheering in a minute," said Bunty, swallow-
ing a sound that indicated other possibilities. "All
right, I'm grateful, you preserved our reputation
most nobly. But if you expect me to live up to your
record, and not ask questions—"

"Wouldn't be any good, darling, I don't know any
more answers."

"Not even who the second ticket was for?"

"That least of all. Because Miles doesn't know it,
either."

"Then I give up! *Why* should he—"

But she stopped there, because there could be
only one reason, and it made her stand back and look
again at young Miles, with sympathy and respect,
and a sudden flurry of consternation and dismay. If
he was reaching after maturity at this rate, without
any childish desire for acknowledgment or payment
or praise, how far behind could Dominic be? She
didn't want them men too soon; she needed a little
time yet to get used to it, even though the symptoms
had begun already so long ago. She caught her
breath in a rueful giggle, and said, "Eve, do you
suppose there's an evening class we could join—on
growing old gracefully?"

She expected something profane and cheering
from Eve in return, but there was blank silence, as
though her friend had withdrawn altogether and cut
off the connection. On Bunty, too, the abrupt chill
of realization descended, freezing her where she
stood.

"Bunty—" said Eve's voice, slowly and delicately.

"Yes, I'm still here. Are you thinking what I'm
thinking?"

"I shouldn't wonder," said Eve. "Great minds!"

"*Could* it be the same person? Since it wasn't Miles, that time—*could* it be? Then anything Miles knows—anything!—may be vital. Anything she ever said to him then, a name or something short of a name. Anything he noticed about her. Anyone he saw her with. She relied on him, she let him help her, she may have trusted him with at least a clue."

"No," said Eve, her voice anxious and still. "Miles doesn't know. *He*—whoever he may be—was always a secret, from Miles, from everybody, just like this time. Terribly like this time, now you come to mention it."

"But there might be something that he does know, without even realizing it. Eve, he must talk to George."

"You took the words out of my mouth. Call me if he shows up there. And if he comes back here," said Eve with grim resolution, *"I'll* see to it that he comes round to your place and gets the whole story off his chest like a sensible man—if I have to bring him along by the ear!"

No one, however, had to bring Miles along by the ear. About seven o'clock Bunty looked out as she drew the living room curtains, and saw them striding briskly and purposefully up the garden path toward the front door, Dominic in the lead. Not merely two young, slender shapes, but three. Somewhere along the way, Bunty thought at first, they'd picked up a third sixth-former who had an uneasy conscience about something he knew and hadn't confided; but when she ran to let them in, and they came into the light of the hall, she saw the third was Tom Kenyon.

Of all people in the world she would least have expected them to run to him for advice. He was too perilously near to them, and yet set apart by the invisible barrier that segregates teacher from pupils; too old to be accepted as a contemporary, and too young to have any of the menace or reassurance of a father figure. They liked him well enough, with reservations, these hard-to-please, deflationary young gentlemen, even if they had christened him Brash 'Arry, jumping to conclusions about the middle initial H. on his briefcase; but to go to him in their anxieties was quite another matter.

"Hallo!" said Bunty, from long habit reducing even the abnormal to normality. "Come in! You're in time for coffee, if you'd like some."

"I'm sorry if we look like an invasion," said Tom, with a brief and shadowed smile, "but this may be urgent. Is George home yet? We've got to see him."

"Yes, come along in." She threw the door wide and passed them through. Her son went by with a single preoccupied glance of apology for his lateness. Miles, always meticulous, said a dutiful, "Good evening, Mrs. Felse!" Tom marshaled them before him with an air of dominant responsibility that made Bunty smile, until she remembered the occasion that had almost certainly brought them here. "Visitors for you, darling!" she said, and closed the door on them and went to reassure Eve.

George had his slippered feet on the low mantelpiece, and his coffee cup in the hearth by his chair. He looked up at their entrance with tired eyes, not yet past surprise at this procession.

"Hallo, Kenyon, what is this? Are you having trouble with these two?"

Two reproving frowns deplored this tone. Tom Kenyon didn't even notice.

"They came to me after they'd seen the paper tonight. It seems they'd been comparing notes and putting two and two together, and they came to the conclusion they had some information and a theory that they ought to confide to somebody in authority. Your boy naturally wanted to come straight to you, but Miles preferred to try it out on me first, before bothering you."

That was one way of putting it. He knew very well why, of course. At first startled and disarmed by their telephone call, he had been tempted to believe that he had done even better than he had supposed during this first term, and established himself as the natural confessor to whom his seniors would turn in trouble. But he had too much good sense to let his vanity run away with him for long. A careful glance at the circumstances, and he knew a better reason. Neither of them would have dreamed of coming to him, if he had not betrayed himself so completely to Miles in that one brief interview. If there was one thing of which Miles was quite certain, after that, it was that Brash 'Arry would be guided in this crisis not by pious thoughts of the good of society or his moral duty, but by one simple consideration: what he felt to be in Annet Beck's best interests. If he listened to their arguments, and then gave it as his opinion that they must go to the police, to the police they would go, satisfied that they were doing the best thing for Annet.

And he needn't think he had the advantage of them as a result of this consultation, either; what it meant, he told himself ruefully but honestly, was that they had discovered in him weaknesses which could be exploited. And boys can be ruthless; he knew, it wasn't so long since he'd been one. They might, on the other hand, be capable of astonishing magnanimity, too. There was stuff in Miles that kept surprising him; his address in this crisis, the direct way he approached his confession, without hesitation or emphasis, the way the "sir" vanished from his tongue, and the greater, not less, respect and assurance that replaced it. Maybe there were things this boy wouldn't use even against a schoolmaster, distresses he wouldn't exploit, even to ease his own.

"I didn't wait to hear all they have to say, but I've heard enough. I said we ought to come straight to you, and tell it at once. So here we are."

Had his own motives, after all, been quite as single and disinterested as they had calculated? Anything that might uncover the identity of Annet's lover he would naturally bring to George at a run, because it might remove the danger that threatened Annet's life. And remove with it, prodded the demon at the back of his mind, the unseen rival, the tenant of that tenacious heart of hers, leaving the way free for another incumbent. He was afraid to look too closely at this dark reverse of his motive, for fear it should prove to be the main impulse that moved him. My God, but it was complicated!

"Sit down!" said George, getting up to pour coffee. "All right, Miles, we're listening. What's on your mind?"

"I've been taking it for granted, of course," said Miles directly, "that I'm on the list of suspects, until you check up on our weekend. Because of the last time. I haven't asked Mr. Kenyon if he knows about that—"

"I do," said Tom.

"—but I know *you* do, of course. And this is going to sound as if I'm just trying to slide out from under, I realize that, but I can't help it."

"Don't let that worry you," said George. "We've already checked, you *are* out from under. We know where you were on Saturday evening, and what you were doing. Just go ahead."

"Oh, good, that makes it easier. You see," said Miles, raising somber brown eyes to George's face in a straight, unwavering stare, "I never did plan to go away anywhere, that last time; it wasn't what it looked like at all. I've never said anything before, and I wouldn't now, except that somebody did plan to go away with her then, and it might—I don't know, but it *might*—be the same person who took her away this time. There's been one murder," said Miles with shattering simplicity, "and there may well be another. Of Annet herself. If we don't find him."

The "we" was significant. He watched George's face, unblinking. "That's right, isn't it?" he said.

"That's right. Go on."

"So we have to find him. And the devil of it is that I didn't try to find out anything about him when I had the chance. I never asked any questions. She asked me to help her to get away. She wanted to go to London. I knew she wasn't happy. I knew they didn't want her to go, and it was wrong, in a way, to help her to leave them high and dry. But she asked me, and I did it. She said her parents would be out when she was supposed to go for her piano lesson in the village that Friday afternoon, and she'd have her cases packed, and would I fetch her and take her to the station at Comerbourne. And I said yes. I'd only just passed my test about three weeks before, I wasn't supposed to touch the car yet unless Dad was with me. But I said yes, anyhow. And I asked her, did she want me to get her ticket for her, so that she could slip in without being noticed at the booking office. And she said it was two tickets she wanted, not one. Singles."

He had paled perceptibly, and for once he lowered

his eyes, frowning down at his own hands clenched tightly in his lap. But only for a moment, while he remustered his forces. "And I booked them for her," he said, "the day before she planned to leave."

"It sounds," said George, carefully avoiding all emphasis, "as though she made fairly shameless use of you."

"No! No, you don't know! It wasn't like that at all. She was perfectly honest with me. I could have said no. I did what I wanted to do. I helped her, and I didn't ask her anything. If she needed to go, as badly as that, I was for her. She didn't owe me anything. And it was for me to choose what I'd do, and I did choose. I booked the tickets for her, and the next day I skipped my last period, and went down to where Dad leaves the car, just round the corner from his office, in the yard at the back. You can't see it from his window, I knew that, and I had the spare key. I fetched Annet and her two cases from Fairford. Her parents were due home in half an hour, but they wouldn't expect her back from her class until six, so she had a couple of hours' grace. I took her to the station. We were a good twenty minutes early, but the train backs in well ahead of time. She said *he* would get on the train independently, with only a platform ticket, and then join her on board. So we went in together when there was a slack moment, and I took a platform ticket from the machine to get out again. We wanted both London tickets punched normally, you see, no queries, nothing to wonder about at all."

"And you never asked her outright who he was? Or even looked round to see if anyone was casing the pair of you? Anyone who might be the boy she was going to meet?"

"No," said Miles, and flamed and paled again in an

instant, remembering stresses within himself that had cost him more than his dignity was prepared to admit.

"All right! This isn't a matter of betrayal now," said George practically, "it's Annet's safety. I believe you didn't ask, I believe you didn't look for him. Leave it at that for now. Go on."

"Well, you know how it ended. Or rather you don't, quite. I meant to have the car back in the yard before Dad ever missed it, and ninety-nine days out of a hundred I could have done it, but that was the hundredth. He had a call from a client who was breaking a train journey for one night at the Station Hotel, and had some bit of business he wanted to clear up quickly. And of course there was no car. He thought it had been stolen—there were several taken around that time, if you remember, locked and everything—some gang going round with a pocketful of keys. Anyhow, he reported it to the police, so after that there wasn't going to be any hushing up the affair, naturally. And then he took a taxi across to the station, and the first thing he saw was his own car parked down at the station approach. Well, of course he tipped off the constable from the corner to keep an eye on it, and he came down to the booking office and the ticket gate to ask if anyone had seen it driven up and parked there. They know him—everybody does. And of course—"

Miles hunched his shoulders under the remembered load.

"That was it! There we were on the platform, with two suitcases, and I had the two tickets in my hand. And he was furious already about the car. I didn't blame him. Actually he was damn decent, considering. But after a bit of publicity like that it was all up with Annet's plans, anyhow. We just let it ride, let him think what he was thinking. We didn't have to consult about it, there wasn't anything else to do. There'd be fuss enough about me, why drag the other fellow into it? All Annet could save out of it was her own secret. Dad said, back to the car, please, and back to the car we went like lambs. He drove out to Fairford, and handed Annet out of the car, and then he looked at the two cases, and neither of them meant a thing to him, but then he never remembers the color of his own from one year to another. Mummy buys them for him, for presents, when the old ones are getting too battered. *He* wouldn't notice. So I handed him one of them, it didn't matter which, and gave Annet the item with one eye, and she caught on at once. Mummy got the other one back to her, afterwards."

"You mean your mother *knew?*" said Tom, startled, his respect for Eve's unwomanly discretion soaring.

"Oh, yes! I don't think it would have taken her long to get the hang of it, anyhow, because Mummy *does* notice things. But she opened the case that same night, meaning to put my things away, so the cat was well and truly out of the bag."

"And she never said a word? Not even to your father?" asked George.

"No, she never did. She could have got me out of some of the muck, of course, but then we'd have had to leave Annet deeper in it, you see, and that was the last thing I wanted. *I* was all right, in any case, my parents never really panic. And at least nobody was pestering Annet about who, or how, or why, the way things were, because they thought they knew. If somebody'd crossed me out they'd have begun on her in earnest. Mummy let me play it my way, and that way there weren't any questions. But you see," said Miles, contemplating his involuntary guilt with set

jaw and dour eyes, "that that makes what's happened since partly my doing. I stood in for him, and
he stayed a secret. She still had him, they could try
again. This time she didn't ask anyone for help, they
didn't risk trains or places where there were people
who might know them. And this time they pulled it
off, if only for a weekend. A trial run for the real
flight, maybe. Only this time," he said with the flat
finality of certainty, "he ran out of funds and killed a
man."

"It doesn't necessarily follow," said George cautiously, "though I admit it's a strong probability."

"I think it does follow. I think if there'd been any
doubt, Annet would have spoken. As soon as she
knew about the murder, she seems to have known
whose life was at stake. Why else should she close
up like this?"

"Even Annet could be wrong," said George. "She
never gave you any clue? You never noticed anything? Saw her with anyone special?"

Miles shook his head decidedly. "Maybe I was
trying not to, I don't know. I've tried all this evening
to dredge up something that might be useful. But
what I have is only deduction. He was from somewhere round here. That's certain, because of the
tickets. She wasn't lying to me about that, I'm sure,
he was going to board the train in Comerbourne.
That time they were bound for London, this time it
was Birmingham. That all ties in. She's never been
away from Comerford for long; it's far more likely
she'd get involved with someone here, someone she
saw often, someone close at home. And someone
hopelessly unsuitable," he said, watching George's
face steadily. "Even more unsuitable than I am now.
I wasn't warned off until after that fiasco. This one,
whoever he is, would never have been allowed near

her at all. That's plain. There was a young follow who drives long-distance lorries. Good-looking chap who danced—"

"We know about him," said George.

"Not that I know anything against him, mind you, only that they wouldn't even have considered him for her. Or there's a clerk from Langford's drawing-office, who used to make trips to London for the firm sometimes. He took her out once or twice, but there are tales about him, and her mother didn't like him, and soon put a stop to it. Someone like that fits the picture. Someone who travels a fair amount and knows his way around. Because *she* doesn't really. With all her assurance, and everything, she's a milk-white innocent."

The urgent, practical, purposeful level of his voice never changed, but suddenly it was sharp with an unbearable concentration of beauty and longing, as though he had charmed Annet into the middle of their close circle. There passed from one to another of them the electric tension of awareness, and every face was taut and still, charged with private anguish. Tom stared sightlessly before him with eyes that had reversed their vision, and were struggling with the uncontrollable apparitions within him. Dominic watched Miles protectively and jealously, and kept his lips closed very firmly upon his personal preoccupations. George saw them momentarily isolated hopelessly one from another. Loneliness is the human condition; we grasp at alleviations where we can find them, but most of the time we have to get by with tenuous illusions of communion. Only families, the lucky ones, and friends, the rare and gifted ones, sometimes grow together and inhabit shared worlds too securely for dispossession.

"And then," pursued Miles, too intent upon his

hunt to be aware of any checks and dismays, even his own, "there's the matter of her reappearance. Nobody seems to have realized how odd that is, and how suggestive."

"And what do you know about her reappearance? There was nothing in the paper about that."

"I know, but Mr. Kenyon began asking us some pretty significant questions the day after half-term, about where we'd been—about where *I'd* been," amended Miles more precisely, "over the weekend, and about the cart road at the back of the Hallowmount. And Mrs. Beck had been on the telephone to my mother, fishing about my whereabouts, too. So we knew there was something wrong at Fairford that *I* should naturally be blamed for unless I had an alibi, and that the track behind the Hallowmount had something to do with it. It *had* to be Annet, or why get after me? But Mr. Kenyon said, when I asked him, that Annet was safe at home. So why all this about the road at the back of the hill, unless they knew she'd gone or come back that way? But that's not all. The grapevine's got it now, with trimmings. Putting all the bits together, and adding what they fancy, as usual. They're saying Annet was found wandering on the Hallowmount at night, and swore she hadn't been anywhere, that she'd only been for a walk and was on her way home. They say she'd been lost to the world for five days under the Hallowmount, like those village girls in the eighteenth century, and remembered nothing about it. They say it in an ambiguous sort of way, if you know what I mean, half believing it really happened, half sniggering over it as a tall tale invented to cover what she was really up to all that time. Round here they're expert in having it both ways." He looked from

George to Tom, and back to George again. "Is it true?"

"Substantially, yes. Mr. Kenyon saw her climb over the Hallowmount on Thursday, and he and her father went up there on Tuesday night, and met her just coming over the crest."

"And she *did* tell that tale? Pretending she knew nothing about the five days in between?"

"Yes," said Tom.

"Then she did it for a pretty urgent and immediate reason. Dom and I have been thinking about this. Nobody knows better than I do," said Miles with authority, "how Annet behaves in a jam like that. I've been through it with her once. She never told a single lie. She walked in at home again with a ruthless sort of dignity, told what she pleased of the truth, and wouldn't say another word. She didn't let me out of it, because I'd shown her I didn't want that. But she never admitted to anything against me, either. She'd have done the same again. That was what she meant to do, I'm certain. If you're thinking she cooked up that tall story as an alibi for the weekend, and turned up on the Hallowmount to give color to it, you're way off target. No, the boot's on the other foot. She told it *because she was caught there.*"

"What you're saying, then," said George intently, "is that Annet was there on the hill for some private and sound reason of her own, and was taken completely by surprise when she came over the crest, intending to go straight home, and ran full tilt into her father and Kenyon."

"Exactly. And she did the best she could with it on the spur of the moment. She'd have done better if she'd had time to think, but she didn't, she had to act instantly. So she fell back on the old tales, not to cover her lost weekend, but to distract attention from what she was doing *there, at that moment.*"

"Go on," said George, after an instant of startling silence that set them all quivering like awakening sleepers. "What do you think, in that case, she *was* doing there?"

"She could," said Dominic, out of the long stillness and quietness he had preserved in his corner, "have been hiding something, for instance. Something neither of them wanted to risk taking home with them."

"Such as?"

"Such as two thousand pounds worth of small jewelry, and what was left of the money after they'd paid their bills."

"No!" protested Tom Kenyon loudly, rigid in his chair. "That's as good as saying she was a party to the crime. I don't believe it. It's impossible!"

"No, sir, I didn't mean that. She needn't have known at all. Suppose he gave her a box, or a small case, or something, and said, here, you keep this safe, it's all I've managed to save, it's our capital. Suppose he told her, Put it somewhere where we can get at it easily when we've made our plans, and are ready to get out of here together. *He*'d know what was really in it, and how completely it could give him away if it was found, but *she* wouldn't, she'd only think he was afraid of his family prying, and getting nosy about his savings, maybe even pinching from them if it happens to be that sort of family. And it easily could. He may be in lodgings, he may have a father who keeps a close watch on him, or scrounging brothers, there could be a dozen reasons why it would be safer to trust to a hiding place in the footways of the old lead mines, or in one of the hollow trees up there, than to risk prying eyes at home. *She* wouldn't know how urgent it really was, but it would make sense even to her. And you see the one solid advantage of putting it somewhere outside rather than having it at either home—if by bad luck it *was* found, there'd be nothing to connect it directly with him. She wouldn't question. She'd do as he asked, and think no wrong until you sprang the murder on her, two days later. *Then* she'd understand."

"In that case, why didn't he persuade her to run at once—permanently—instead of coming home at all? He had the girl, he had the money. Why not make off with them both while he had the chance?"

"Because he was comfortably sure there was nothing in the world to connect him with the murder, and to run without reason just at that time would have been the quickest way of inviting suspicion. Wouldn't it?" challenged Dominic earnestly, brilliant eyes clinging to his father's face.

"You're forgetting," said Tom, "the roaming Romeo who tried to pick her up." He caught himself up too late, and met George's eye in embarrassed dismay. "I'm sorry, probably I shouldn't have mentioned that. It hasn't been published, has it?"

"It hasn't, but since we seem to have embarked on a fullscale review, it may as well be." He recounted the episode briefly. "There's certainly a point there. When he heard of that incident he'd know there was a possible witness who'd be able to tie in Annet, at least, to the scene and time of the murder. It isn't difficult to give a recognizable description of Annet. It would be impossible not to recognize any decent photograph of her, once you'd seen her at close quarters."

"But she wouldn't know there was any urgent reason to warn him that a witness existed, because she knew of no crime. And without an urgent reason," said Miles with absolute and haughty certainty, "she wouldn't say a word to him about a thing like that."

"Not tell him, when she'd been accosted by a streetcorner lout?"

The very assumption of intimate knowledge of her, even at this extremity of her distress and need, could prick both these unguarded lovers into irritation and jealousy. Kenyon had allowed himself to slip into the indulgent schoolmaster voice that brought Miles's hackles up; Miles was staring back at him with the aloof and supercilious face that covers the modern sixth-former's wilder agonies. The minute action and reaction of pain quivered between them, and made them contemporaries, whether they liked it or not. Dominic's very acute and intelligent eyes studied them both from beneath lowered lashes, and what he felt he kept to himself. But the air was charged with sympathy and antagonism in inseparable conflict, and for a moment they all flinched from the too strident discord of the clash.

"No," said Miles, more gently but no less positively. "It was a thing she wouldn't confide. Especially not to him."

"Well, if you're right about that, he'd have no idea that there was going to be anyone to give a description of either of them. He knew he'd left no traces, he thought he was quite clear. Every reason why he should hope to lie low for a reasonable time, and let the robbery in Birmingham blow over. Yes, that makes sense," agreed George. "It seems possible that he may not even have known, at first, that the old man was dead. Most probably he hit and grabbed and ran, and left him, as he thought, merely knocked out."

"And even when he knew it was murder, there was nothing, as far as he knew, to connect him with it. The obvious thing to do was come inconspicuously home again, and go back to work, and act normally. Hide the money and the jewelry," pursued Dominic, returning to his trail tenaciously, "or get Annet to hide them, somewhere where naturally he hoped they'd stay safely hidden, but where at any rate they couldn't incriminate him any more than anyone else if they were discovered. But now it's gone past that. There *was* a witness he didn't know about, and Annet *has* been identified. The case is tied firmly to Annet and the man who spent the weekend with her. And only Annet's resistance stands between him and a murder charge. That's the situation he finds himself in now."

"There's another point." Miles frowned down at the hands that had tightened almost imperceptibly on each other at every repetition of her name, and carefully, painfully disengaged them. "Supposing this is a good guess of ours, and she was entrusted with the business of hiding the money, then of course they may have agreed on the place beforehand. It may even be a place they've used for other things before now. But it may not. Supposing nobody but Annet knows where the stolen jewelry and money is now? He knows his life depends on her keeping silent. If he gets to the point of being terrified into running for it, he can't even get his loot and run without contacting Annet. And if he does—"

"He can't," George said reassuringly. "We've got a constant guard on her, inside the house and out. The degree of her danger hasn't escaped us. And we don't intend to take our eyes off her. You can rely on that."

"Yes—" And he was grateful, a pale smile pierced the preoccupied stillness of his face for a moment.

"But he's got nothing to lose now unless he can get the means to make his break. And if he can find a way to her somehow, he's liable to remember that she—that nobody else can identify him—"

Miles carefully moistened lips suddenly too dry to finish the sentence.

"Yes, I realize all that. But I've got a man outside the house, Miles, and a policewoman inside with her. And however desperate he may be, we're dealing with only one man. The essence of his situation is that he's alone."

"Not quite alone," said Miles inaudibly. "He's got one person who might help him to get to her, if ever you so much as turn your back for a minute."

George stood off and looked down at him heavily, and said never a word in reply to that. It was Tom Kenyon, still fretting against the arrogance of the boy's certainty, who demanded: "Who's that?"

"Annet," said Miles.

They had talked themselves into dead silence. The two boys sat with the width of the room between them, braced and still, their eyes following with unwavering attention every quiver of George's brooding face, while he told over again within his mind the points they had made, and owned their substance. They had good need to be afraid for Annet, and very good reason to look again and again at the looming, significant shape of that long hogback of rock and rough pasture that linked her with and divided her from her lover. Was it necessarily true that Annet had had a particular purpose in being on the Hallowmount that night of her return? Wasn't it simply her road back? Wasn't it natural enough that they should use the same route returning as departing? She wouldn't be afraid of the Hallowmount in the dark. But in that case, according to Miles, she wouldn't have troubled to cover herself and her movements with that fantastic story, even when she was taken by surprise on top of the hill. She drew her veil of deception because she had something positive and precise to hide. Who should know better than Miles?

But even if she had indeed been entrusted with the hiding of the plunder on her way home, was it likely that she had put it somewhere unknown to her partner? Possible, at a stretch, but certainly not likely. What appeared to George every moment more probable was that they had some hiding place already established between them, and frequently used, their letter box, their private means of communication, accessible from both sides of the mountain without difficulty and without making oneself conspicuous. Given such a cache, tested and found reliable from long use, it would not even occur to them to hide their treasure anywhere else. And it would be the most natural thing in the world for Annet to undertake the job of depositing it, if the spot was directly on her way home. The boy had his motorbike to manage, and his own family to manipulate at home; and by consent, so it seemed, they made use of the Hallowmount as the watershed of their lives, and the act of crossing it alone had become a rite. It was the barrier between their real and their ideal worlds, between the secret life they shared and the everyday life in which their paths never touched, or never as lovers. It was the hollow way into the timeless dream place, as surely as if the earth had opened and drawn them within.

What was certain was that they had between them a treasure to hide. What was likely was that they had a place proved safe by long usage, in which to hide it. What was left to question was whether it was still there. Up to the appearance of the evening paper, probably he had no reason to see any urgency in its recovery, and every reason to avoid going near it. But now?

For some hours now he had known how closely he was hunted. Frightened, inexperienced, unable to confide in or rely on anyone but himself, how long would it take him to make up his mind? Or how long to panic? He might well have retrieved the money already. But he might not. And whether they were justified in all these deductions or not, there was nothing to be lost by keeping a watch on the Hallow-mount, in case he did betray himself by making for his hoard. Heaven knew they had no other leads to him, except the mute girl in Fairford.

Price wouldn't thank him for a chilly, solitary night patrolling the border hills, but anything was worth trying. George excused himself, and went to telephone. When he came back into the room none of them had moved. They all looked up at him expectantly.

"I'm putting a man on watch overnight," said George, "in case he goes to recover it during the dark hours. You may very well be right about it being hidden there, somewhere on the hill. Night's the most likely time for him to go and fetch it, if by any chance he does know where to look, but covering the ground by daylight won't be so easy. The last thing I want to do is put him off, and the sight of a plainclothes man parading the top of the Hallow-mount would hardly be very reassuring. And man-power," he owned, dubiously gnawing a knuckle, "isn't our long suit."

"We could provide you with boypower," said Tom Kenyon unexpectedly. "Plenty of it, and it might be a pretty good substitute. Miss Darrill's taking out the school Geographical Association on one of their occasional free-for-alls tomorrow. They were having a field day on Cleave, but there's no reason why they couldn't just as well be switched to the Hallowmount. It's geologically interesting, it would carry conviction, all right. And if we deploy about forty boys all over the hill it will make dead certain nobody can hunt for anything there without being spotted. As well as giving us three a chance to do some hunting on our own. If you gentlemen," said Tom, looking his two sixth-formers in the eye with respectful gravity, "wouldn't mind joining in for the occasion?"

They had stiffened and brightened, they looked back at him as at a contemporary, measuring and eager, only a little wary.

"If it would be any help?" said Miles, casting a questioning glance at George. "And if you think we should involve Miss Darrill? We should have to tell her why."

"It would give me a day," said George, "the most important day, the day he's likely to break. He knows now how he stands. Of course Miss Darrill must know what's in the wind, but nobody else, mind. And if she does consent, she's to do nothing whatever except what she was going out to do, take her members on a field expedition and keep them occupied in a perfectly normal way. All I need is that you should be there, and prevent him from getting near any possible hiding place on the hill. If he's collected his loot already, it can't be helped. But if he hasn't, that's our only working lead to him."

"Jane will do it," said Tom positively. "And what if we should find the stuff ourselves? What do we do?"

"You leave it where it is, but don't let the spot out

of your sight, I'm going to have to be in Birmingham
part of the day, but before the daylight goes I'll be
ready to relieve you. Can you hold the fort until
then?"

"Yes, until you come, whenever that is." It was the
only way he had of helping Annet. She might not be
grateful, she might hate him for it, but there was no
other way.

"Good! I'll try to be back in the station by four-
thirty. Will you call me there then? If anything
breaks earlier, I'll get word to you as soon as I
usefully can."

"I'll do that. And may I call Jane Darrill now?
Better give her what warning we can, if we're
upsetting her bus arrangements."

He called her, and the light, assured, faintly amused
voice that answered him manifested no surprise.
Curious that he should be able to hear in it, over the
telephone, wry overtones of reserve and doubt he
had never noticed in it in their daily encounters.

"That means switching tea to somewhere in Comerford," she said, sighing. "There won't be time to
take them out to the Border. And what do you
suppose the Elliots will do with the provisions laid
in for forty hungry boys?"

"I didn't think about that," he said, dismayed.
"Well, if you can't do it, of course—"

"Who said I couldn't do it? Twenty-four hours'
notice is required only for the impossible. Don't
worry, I live here, I can fix tea, all right. By the way,
who's asking me to do this, you or the police?"

"Me," he said simply, without even the affectation
of correctness.

"Just as long as we know," said Jane, a shade
dryly. "All right, it's on."

She hung up the receiver, and left him troubled by

tensions newly discovered in himself, when he had
thought that Annet had exhausted all his resources
of feeling and experience. He wondered, too, as he
went back to report to George in the living room,
why he should feel ashamed, but he had no leisure to
indulge his desire to examine the more obscure
recesses of his own mind. There had been, through-
out, only one person who really mattered, and for the
first time in his life it was not himself.

"That's that," he said. "It's arranged. I think we'd
better call it a day now, if we're going to be on patrol
between us all day tomorrow. Come on, Miles, I'll
run you home."

In the hall he hung back and let the boys go out
into the chill of the night ahead of him. There was
still something he had to ask George. He could not
remember ever feeling so responsible for any boy in
his charge as he did now for Miles; the act of
confiding had drawn them closer than he found quite
comfortable, and probably the boy was chafing, too.

"It's definite, isn't it?" he asked in a low voice, as
they emerged on the doorstep. "What you said about
young Mallindine? They were up there in Snowdonia
the whole time?"

"Quite definite. We've already checked on their
weekend." George remembered the mental clip over
the ear that was in store for Dominic when the time
was ripe, and smiled faintly in the dark. The two
boys were talking in low tones, out there beside the
Mini, small, taut, tired voices studiously avoiding
any show of concern with the things that really filled
their minds. "Don't worry about them, they're in the
clear."

"I shouldn't think you've ever been so glad to cross
off your prime suspect," said Tom, feeling his own
heart lift perceptibly, even in its passionate preoc-

cupation with that other hapless young creature for
whom there was no such relief.

"Well, he wasn't that, exactly, he was rather down
the list, as a matter of fact. Though as it turns out,"
said George with soft deliberation, "we've lost Number One as well."

"You have? Who—?" But perhaps he wasn't allowed to ask; it was all too easy to assume that good
will entitled you to the confidence of the authorities.
"Sorry, I take that back. Naturally you can't very
well talk about it."

"Oh, in this case I think I could." George cast one
brief glance at him along his shoulder, and saw the
young, good-looking, self-confident face paler and
more thoughtful than usual, but unshakable in innocence and secure as a rock. "Number One was an
obvious case for investigation. In close contact with
her daily, then clean away from here for the weekend just as she vanished. Involved closely in her
reappearance, too, as if he knew where to look for
her, and was interested in creating the atmosphere
for her return. Anxious to be around when I began to
ask questions, very anxious to know the odds. And
falling over himself to point out to me indications
that someone else had been on the scene."

Tom was staring back at him blankly, searching
his mind in all the wrong directions, and still quite
unable to see this eligible lover anywhere in the
case.

"But there wasn't anyone. The trouble from the
beginning was that there was no one in close contact
with her like that—"

"No one?" said George with a hollow smile. "Yes,
there was this one fellow. Right age, right type, and
rubbing shoulders with her every day. You mean to
say you never noticed him? But we've checked up on

his movements all the weekend, too, and he's well and truly out of it. He went home like a lamb, just as he said he was going to, and he was in a theater with another girl when Jacob Worrall was killed. For God's sake!" said George between irritation and respect, "do you want me to tell you what they saw?"

Then it came, the full realization, like a weight falling upon Tom and flattening the breath out of him. He froze in incredulous shock, heels braced into the gravel, staring great-eyed through the dark and struggling for words, confounded by this plain possibility which had never once occurred to him. What sort of complacent fool had he been? He stood off now and looked at himself from arm's length, with another man's eyes; and that, too, was a new experience to him.

"You mean to say you never realized? Why do you suppose I asked Dr. Thorpe to stay with Annet, that night, until my man came to keep watch on her? Who else knew at that time that we were on to her? Who else could have known that she was a threat to him? Did you think I was protecting her from her father? You weren't a very likely murderer in yourself," said George gently, propelling the stricken young man along the path toward the waiting boys, "and you could hardly have been her partner in that first attempt at fight, six months ago, that's true. But even now it isn't by any means certain that the man we're looking for is the same person, it's merely a fair probability. And on circumstantial evidence alone, until Miss MacLeod put you clean out of the reckoning today, you were undoubtedly Number One."

CHAPTER 8

GeORGE came to Fairford very early in the morning, intent on being unexpected, appearing when Annet was still in a housecoat, pale and silent and unprepared for the renewed assault. But it seemed there was no time of the day or night when she was not armed against him and everyone. Her great eyes had swallowed half her face, the fine, clear flesh was wasting away alarmingly from her slender bones. She looked as if she had not slept at all, as if she had stared into the dark unceasingly all through the night, gazing through her window at the ridge of the Hallowmount, stretched like a slumbering beast against the eastern sky.

He asked her the old questions, and she was silent with the old silence, patient and absolute. He sat down beside her and told her, in clipped, quiet tones, everything he knew about Jacob Worrall's narrow, harmless, shabby life, about his poor little backroom hobby of collecting local Midland porcelain, about the two blows that had splintered his fragile skull and spilled his meager, old-man's blood

over the boards of his workroom. He chose words
that made her tremble, and pushed them home like
knives, but she never gave him word or sound in
return. The room was full of pain, but the only words
were his words. He wanted to stop, but she had to
speak, she had to be made to speak.

It occurred to him at length, and why he did not
know, to send Policewoman Crowther out of the
room, to wait below until he should call her back. As
soon as the door had closed behind her Annet leaned
and took his hand and smoothed it between hers,
entreating him with clinging, frantic fingers and
desperate eyes.

"Let me go!" Her voice was only a breath between
her lips, a small, broken sound. She held his hand to
her cheek, and the drift of her dark hair flowed over
it. "Take her away from me, take them all away, and
let me go! Oh, please, please, take them all away and
leave me alone!"

"No, Annet, I can't do that. You know I can't."

How well Miles knew her, and how deeply he
understood the real threat to her now. Whether she
understood what she was trying to do was another
matter. All George was sure of was that he had only
to remove all restrictions from her, and sit back and
watch, and she would lead him to her lover; and that
he could not let her do it, that he would not risk her
even to catch a murderer. He could not make her
speak, and she could not make him grant her the
freedom of action she wanted, to throw her own life
away after the old man's life.

"You must! Please! I've done nothing. Let me go!
You must let me go!"

"No."

"Then there's nothing I can do, nothing, nothing—

Oh, please help me! Help me! Take everyone away and let me go free!"

The dark hair slipped away on both sides to uncover the tender nape of her neck, and its child-ishness and fragility was more than he could bear. He took his hand from her almost roughly, and walked out of the room, and her long, shuddering sigh of despair followed him down the stairs.

"No," he said wearily, meeting her mother's questioning eyes in the doorway of the living room. "Hasn't she said anything to you that could offer us a lead?"

"She says nothing to me. She might be struck dumb. She's like this with everyone."

"And no one's asked to see her? Or to speak to her on the telephone?"

"Not to speak to her, no. The vicar rang up to ask after her. And Regina, of course." Even in this extremity she could not suppress the little, proud lift of her voice, at being on Christian name terms with Mrs. Blacklock of Cwm Hall. "Last night, that was, after the papers came. She and Peter were both very distressed about her. They asked if there was anything they could do, and if they could come and see her. I told them you didn't wish anyone to see her yet. Though she isn't charged with anything," said Mrs. Beck, staring him hard in the eye, "and we have a right if we choose—"

"Of course you have. But you also have the good sense to understand the sound reasons why you should listen to me and do what I say. When you stop agreeing with me, let them all in," said George patiently.

"We know you have a job to do, of course. And I suppose it gives an impression of activity to mount guard on my girl, when there's nothing else you can think of doing. Naturally you want to keep up your reputation—"

"What I chiefly want," said George, walking past her to the door, "is to keep Annet alive."

He went out into the bright air of morning, and the sun was high above the Hallowmount, climbing in a sky washed clean of clouds. Thank God for a fine Saturday for Jane Darrill's field day with the Geographical Association. No one would wonder too much at seeing forty small boys let loose over the hills on a sunny October afternoon, no one, not even themselves, would suppose they were there to fend off a thief and murderer from recovering his gains (if, of course, he had not already recovered them), and no one would think that even their supervisors and elders were looking for anything more sensational than samples of the local flora, and of the conglomerates, grits and slates of the ridge, or the occasional fragment of galena, or bright bits of quartzite from the outcrop rocks.

Thanks to them, George thought as he slammed the door of the car and drove along the lane to Wastfield, he had this one day's grace; and it hung heavy upon his mind that that was all he had, and that he must make it bear fruit. Time trod so close and crushingly on his heels that he had difficulty now in remembering that the murder of Jacob Worrall was, in the first place, Birmingham's case and not his.

He had extracted a list of Annet's closest school friends from her mother; he checked it with Myra Gibbons, who had been closest even among these, and she supplied, with some encouragement, details of their subsequent whereabouts and fortunes. It

might be time wasted, but it might not. No one had yet provided any clue as to where Annet and her partner had spent their nights in Birmingham, though by this time the hotels were all eliminated, and even the bed and breakfast places dwindling. One of Annet's G.C.E. class, it seemed, was now reading English literature at Birmingham University, and another was studying at the School of Art. Probably both in respectable supervised lodgings, but sometimes they found flatlets which afforded them privacy enough to abuse the privilege. And even if they had not given her a bed, they might have been in touch with Annet while she was there. No need for them to have seen the boy, he could easily be kept in the background. But even there, there was at least a chance.

He telephoned Duckett from the box at the edge of the village, and reported his meager gains: three addresses where there might be something to be gleaned, the two girl students, and an old, retired teacher who had once been on unusually good terms with the fourteen-year-old Annet at the Girls' High School in Comerbourne.

"They'd have come forward," said Duckett positively, "if they'd known anything about her moves. The teacher, anyhow."

"You would think so. But we can't afford to miss anything. Have you talked to them again at that end? I take it they've got nothing?"

"Nothing? Boy, they've got everything, except what they want. The usual lunatic fringe ringing up from everywhere else but the right places, reporting having seen everybody but the right girl. They creep out from under every stone," said Duckett bitterly, "and run to the nearest telephone. But no sense so far. And yet they must have slept somewhere. And even

with dark glasses and a different hairdo and whatever, you couldn't hide that girl every minute of the
day. Somewhere in the ladies' room of a café she'd be
sure to redo her hair, somewhere she'd take off her
hat, if she was wearing one."

"I don't believe she ever tried to disguise herself,"
said George. "She was committing only a private sin,
and she wasn't ashamed or afraid, once she was
away from Comerford, once she'd got what she
wanted. I don't believe she ever even tried very hard
to hide from anyone. If she had, she might have been
noticed more. And yet, as you say, they slept somewhere, they ate somewhere. Public transport they
didn't need, if they had the motorbike. And if they
walked the streets together, they did it in the dark.
The two witnesses who came forward and identified
her as the girl on the corner wouldn't have been
much use to us, either, if she hadn't stood under a
streetlight."

"As you say. For one who wasn't trying, she made
a pretty good job of being invisible."

"Agreed, but largely accidentally. You see she
didn't mind being seen that night. She did stand
under a light, she didn't try to withdraw even when
the Brummie lad came along, she only froze him out
when he got too oncoming. She didn't know of any
more pressing reason for hiding herself or her lover
than the mere preservation of their weekend together. But somehow the circumstances of their stay
in the town were such that they did remain unnoticed. That's how I read it."

"You could be right," said Duckett. "Try it out."

"Nothing new? Has Scott reported anything further on Geoff Westcott?"

A spurt of laughter exploded in George's ear.

Duckett laughing meant trouble for someone, but decidedly not hanging trouble.

"Has he! And very interesting it all is, too, but I doubt if it'll do much for you, George. No, the thing is, Geoff told Scott yesterday he'd been down in South Wales with that side-kick of his, Smoky Brown, staying with Smoky's cousins in Gower. Said the whole clan would bear him out. Scott didn't doubt that, knowing our Browns, so he didn't ask 'em, he went straight to Martha Blount, before Geoff could get away from Lowthers' last night. Told her Geoff had told him he'd traveled south for the weekend with *the Browns,* to stay with their cousins, and asked her if she could confirm it. Innocent style, she'd be sure to know, and all that. And Smoky Brown's sister being the only other Brown in the reckoning, and a very hot little number into the bargain, Martha jumped to the inevitable conclusion, and all but went through the roof. The rat, she says, so *that's* what he meant by doing a long-distance driving job as a favor to a friend! And me believing every word, like a damned fool! All Scott had to do was put in the right questions whenever she stopped for breath: What friend? Where to? What was he carrying? She came out with everything he'd told her, and what he'd told her was the truth as far as it went, and it went one hell of a long way. He didn't tell her where they'd lifted all the lead from, but would you believe it, he told her in confidence where he was delivering it. Two trips, two lorry loads, to a back-street yard in Bolton. Love's a terrible thing."

"Doesn't mix with business, anyhow," agreed George wryly. "Think they'll be in time to pick up the goods?"

"With luck, yes. How are the receivers to know

he'd be such a fool as to tell his girl the real reason why he couldn't take her out Saturday? Didn't tell her his cargo was pinched, of course, but he only pulled himself up just short of that."

So that was another one off the list of possibilities, thought George as he hung up the receiver. Poor Martha! But at least if she made up her mind she was well rid of Geoff, no one was going to die of it. And if she cut her losses and made the best of him, with her force of character she might keep him out of jail in future. Once having told her the truth, it wouldn't be any use telling her lies thereafter; she would always be on the lookout and ready to shorten the rein. And if young Geoff really wanted her, as seemed, oddly enough, a strong possibility, he must have thrown such a scare into himself this time that he'd do almost anything in future rather than take the risk of losing her again. She might, even, find it easy to forgive him and wait for him, in the relief of finding that he was not unfaithful, but merely a minor criminal.

Their small story, at least, need not occupy him. A few more such intrusive comedies, and his list of possibles would be dwindling out of sight.

He drove through Comerford and over the bridge, and round the eastern flank of the long, triple-folded range to Cwm Hall. The long drive unrolled before him, the vista of the park and the hollow square of the stableyard over to the left, aside from the house and by two centuries younger. To the rear of the beautiful, E-shaped house lay the farm buildings, barns and dovecote so tall that they showed above the mellow red roofs.

Regina was at her desk in one of the large windows, ploughing her way remorselessly through her morning's correspondence without Annet's aid. She

saw the car sweep round the wide curve of the drive
to halt on the apron of gravel, and waved a hand and
rose at once to come out to George on the doorstep.

"Mr. Felse, I'm so glad to see you. I've been
longing to telephone Mrs. Beck again, but it seems
cruel to pester the poor woman." The alert, com-
manding blue eyes looked a little startled behind the
distorting lenses of her reading glasses. The brisk-
ness and decision of her movements and words,
undaunted by death, suspicion or suffering, sprang
to meet him almost roughly; no wonder those on
whom she conferred her quite genuine visitations of
sympathy often reacted with bristling hackles and
tongue-tied offense. And yet she was a kind, sincere
woman, and the one thing she would not do for those
in distress or need was leave them gently, self-
sacrificingly alone.

"Do tell me about Annet. This is such a terrible
business, I don't understand how she *could* have
become involved. We were always so careful of her.
And she isn't a deceitful child by nature, I'm sure
she isn't, there was never any signs. How *could* we
have failed to see that there was someone on her
mind? How is the poor girl now?"

"Physically," said George, bracing himself and
digging in his heels against the force of her energy,
"she's well enough."

"You don't want us to see her yet? I don't want to
make things more difficult for you in any way, but do
let us know as soon as we can go to her. We're very
concerned. If there's anything we can do in the
meantime, please do ask, we should be very glad if
we could help her."

So would a great many people, thought George,
remembering Tom Kenyon and Miles Mallindine
eyeing each other across his rug in an anguish

bitterly antagonistic and helplessly shared. Some
with better rights even than yours.

"Do you want to talk to Peter? He's down in the
stableyard with Stockwood, I think, working on one
of the cars."

"It's with Stockwood I wanted to have a word, as a
matter of fact."

"Oh!" she said, drawing back a step to measure
him with blue eyes wide and wary. "I thought he'd
already satisfied you about his movements. One of
your men was here yesterday afternoon to talk to
him."

"I know. Just a detail I'd like to check with him
myself. If you've no objection?"

"I have no objection, of course. But I think I
should tell you that I feel every confidence in this
young man. I haven't had him long, that's true, but I
can usually make up my mind fairly soon about
people. I see," she said with authority, "why you
must consider him as a possibility. But I'm sure
you'll be wasting your time."

"He's simply one man who at least has been in
occasional contact with Annet. You must take my
word for it that that's enough to make this necessary."

"And personable," said Regina, suddenly running
her fingers deep into the orderly waves of her short
red hair, and clenching them there for a moment.
"And young!"

The faint, astonished tang of bitterness the word
had for her made her mouth twist. Had she looked
too often and too closely at the chauffeur herself? It
wouldn't be the first time that had happened to a busy,
self-confident, indulgent woman suddenly shocked
into awareness that youth had left her. If so, she had
surely never done more than look; she was too
certain of herself to sacrifice a part of her personal-

ity to an employee, whatever the momentary temptations.

"How much more do you know about him? He came to you with references, of course?"

"One," she said, "from his last employer, a businessman down in Richmond. But of course you can see the letter if you want to. Before that he says he was in Canada for a year, driving or doing any job he could get. So far we've found him completely satisfactory."

It was a royal "we," and George recognized it as such; Peter had no use for a chauffeur, and no interest in this one provided Regina was happy.

"Oh, I don't doubt that. And he lives in Braidie's old quarters?"

"In the south lodge." It was behind the house, and hidden from it by the older plantations Peter had brought to such excellent growth and condition.

"Alone? Or is he a married man?"

"He has been married. His wife got a divorce from him—at least, it won't be absolute for a month or so yet. Over an incident with another woman. You see, he was very frank with me about his circumstances when he applied for the job."

"So he does live alone?" In that minor lodge on a very quiet road, out of sight of the house, where coming and going would be easy. "And does for himself?"

"Yes, very economically and neatly, so I'm told." She smiled for an instant, but wryly. "Our head gardener has a rather forward daughter who has made it her business to offer her services, but she hasn't got anywhere so far. He doesn't seem to have any use for women, by all the signs."

No, maybe not. But then he wouldn't, for other women, if he had Annet in his sights.

"I'll go round and join them, if I may."

"Do, of course. You know your way."

George walked round the wing of the house and down the slope of grass. The eighteenth-century stable block sat four-square about a large courtyard, two-storyed, many-windowed, like a mansion in itself. There were still three riding horses in the place, but the cars had nearly elbowed them out of their own yard. Peter Blacklock, in slacks and an old polo-necked sweater, was bending into the hood of the E-type Jaguar that was credibly reputed to be Regina's last birthday present to him. Stockwood, in overalls, was washing down the Bentley. He turned his head at the hollow sound of footsteps under the stable archway, and showed that proud, dark face of his, withdrawn and defensive as a Romany. For a moment he was motionless. Water streamed from his rubber brush down the flanks of the car, and flowed away into the drain.

Peter Blacklock took his head out of the car's innards, and shook back the lank fair hair from his forehead with a nervous toss of his head.

"Oh, hallo, Felse!" Something of consternation, something of resignation, showed in his long, hyper-sensitive features for an instant, and then was gone as suddenly, leaving only his usual faintly weary but beautifully modulated politeness. "I'm sorry, I didn't hear you come. Were you looking for me?"

He leaned into the car and switched off the purring engine, and stood wiping his hands on a tangle of cotton-waste. "Am I allowed to ask about Annet? We've been—we *are* terribly anxious about her. There's nothing new?"

"No, nothing new." He didn't want to talk to anyone about Annet, he didn't want to show to anyone else even a part of what she had made him experience. "We're still filling in details wherever and however we can—about all the people we can. Do you mind if I ask Stockwood a few questions?"

"If you must," said Peter, frowning. "But I thought you'd already done with him. He accounted for himself to one of your fellows yesterday. Something the matter with the liaison, or what?"

"Nothing the matter with the liaison. Just a double check for safety's sake. And you might fill in the timing of the weekend for me yourself first, if you will. Mrs. Blacklock went off to Gloucester on the Thursday afternoon. Stockwood drove her down and brought back the car, because she was meeting a friend there who could run her about locally. You then gave him the whole long weekend off, I understand. Exactly when did he leave here, and when did he return?"

In the very brief moment of quietness Stockwood leaned and turned off the tap. He laid down the brush and took a step toward them, waiting in readiness, dark color mounting in his face and blanching again to pallor.

"He garaged the car about a quarter to five," said Peter in a thin, brittle voice, his long face sagging with reluctance and distress. "I told him he could consider himself free until the following Wednesday noon, and then come in for the Bentley and fetch my wife home. I told him if he liked he could make use of one of the B.S.A.s for his weekend, and he said yes, he would like to. I don't know what time he left the lodge, but it was all in darkness before six o'clock. He came back prompt at noon on Wednesday, and drove to Gloucester to bring Regina back."

"You didn't ask him where he was going?"

"I didn't. I don't. Nor where he'd been, when he came back. He's my wife's employee, not mine, but even if he were mine I shouldn't think that gave me any right to ask him where he spends his free time. Only his working hours are bought and paid for." He added gently and wearily, "Your business, of course, it may very well be. *You* ask him."

The young man dried his hands carefully, automatically, confronting them both with a wary face and narrowed eyes. He had left it too late to protest at being interrogated again, and far too late to pretend surprise or indignation. He waited, moistening his lips, a glitter in his eyes that might have been anger, but looked closer kin to desperation.

"I think," said George after a moment of thought, "I'd better talk to Stockwood alone. If you don't mind?"

Blacklock did mind, that was abundantly clear; he felt a degree of responsibility for all the members of his wife's staff, and was reluctant to abandon any of them to the mercies of the police, however implicit his faith might be, in theory, in British justice. He hesitated for a moment, swung on his heel to pick up his jacket from the stone bench in the middle of the yard.

"All right! I'll see you when you've finished, Felse. Look in at the house for a moment if I'm not around, will you?"

He went out through the deep archway between the coach houses with his long, nervous stride, and vanished up the slope of the field toward the hall.

"Well?" said George. "Where *did* you spend the weekend?"

The young man drew breath carefully between lips curled in detestation and fright. "I've told you already. I told your bloke who was here yesterday—"

"You told him you went to a fishing inn up the

Teme valley—I know. Not having a home of your own to go to."

Stockwood's head jerked back; the gypsy face took fire in a brief blaze of defiance quickly suppressed.

"You thought the landlord was a friend of yours, and quick on the uptake, and would see you through. Maybe he promised you he would, when you phoned him. Maybe he really would, up to a holdup or a smash-and-grab. But as soon as he smelled murder he packed it in. He's not getting lumbered with any part of it, boy. And you weren't at the Angler's Arms last Saturday night. So where were you?"

The color had ebbed from Stockwood's face so alarmingly that it seemed there could not be enough blood in him to keep his heart working. George took him by the arm and sat him down, unresisting, on the stone bench. The lean young face, self-conscious and proud, stood him off steadily; and in a moment the blanched lines of jaw and mouth eased.

"That's better. Take it quietly. It's very simple. You gave us a phony tale about where you spent your free weekend. Now all I want is the truth, and for your own sake you'd better produce it. You'd have done better," he said dryly, "to stick to it in the first place, when you came here after the job. Why didn't you tell Mrs. Blacklock you had a prison record? Oh, no, I haven't told her, either, so far this is just between you and me. But you must have cased the job and the people before you tried it, you should have been able to judge that she'd take you even with a stretch behind you—maybe all the more."

"I didn't know," said the young man through tight lips. "How could I? I wanted the job, and I was on the level. I didn't dare to risk what she'd do if she knew."

"I'm telling you, she'd have taken you on just the same. She'd pride herself on giving you your chance."

"That's what you fellows always say. And that's what women like her always say. But when it came to the point how could I be sure? I've done the job properly," he said, stiffening his neck arrogantly, and stared up into George's face without blinking. "Didn't take your lot long to get after my record, did it?"

"It doesn't, once we've got the idea, once we know you're lying about your movements last weekend. We can connect. It doesn't follow," said George, "that we think you necessarily did the Bloome Street job. It's a long way from helping to hijack a load of cigarettes to killing a man. But nobody lies about his movements without having something to hide. So where were you?"

Stockwood's jaw clamped tight to shut in whatever words he might have been about to blurt out furiously in George's face. He sat for a moment with his hands clenched and braced on the edge of the stone seat. There was no hope of success with a second lie, and all too clearly he had no new line of defense prepared. After a brief struggle his lips opened stiffly, and said abruptly, "With a woman."

"Miss Beck?" said George conversationally.

"*No, not* Miss Beck!"

"Rosalind Piper again?"

Or was it "still" rather than "again"? But there was as little reason for him to hide a connection with her as there was to continue or resume it. According to the records, she had cost him a year in jail by involving him in the gang in the first place; and she had cost him his marriage, too, it seemed, since there was a divorce hanging over him. Briefly George wondered what she had looked like. A blonde

decoy with a brazen face, or a little innocent creature with big blue eyes? The boy could have been
only about twenty-one or twenty-two at the time,
and not long married, probably a decent enough
young man with good prospects, but the usual,
ever-present money difficulties; and a quick share-
out from one big haul must have seemed to him an
enticing proposition, especially the way the experienced Miss Piper had pictured it for him, with
herself as a bonus.

"No!" Stockwood spat the negative after her memory, and turned his head obstinately away.

"I have no interest," said George patiently, "in
your private affairs, as long as you're breaking no
laws. You'd better give her a name. If she bears you
out, I can forget it." If she bore him out, it would be
the truth.

"*You* might," said Stockwood. "*She* wouldn't."

"If she didn't grudge you the weekend, she won't
grudge you an alibi. What harm can there be in
asking her to confirm your story? If, of course, it's
true this time."

"It's true!"

"And if you did nothing the law would be interested in."

"No. I didn't do anything wrong. You won't be able
to prove I did, because I didn't."

"Then don't be a fool. Tell me who she is, and help
yourself and me."

"No—I can't tell you!"

"You'll have to in the end. Come on, now, she won't
be inconvenienced, we have no interest in her. But
unless you name her you're putting yourself in a
nasty spot, and casting doubt on every word you
have told me."

"I can't help it," said Stockwood stubbornly, and

licked a trickle of sweat from his lips. "I can't tell you."

"You can't because she's as big a lie as the fishing weekend. She doesn't exist."

"She does exist! Oh, my God!" He said it in a sudden, soft, hopeless voice to himself, as though, indeed, she was the only creature who did exist for him, and of her reality he was agonizingly unsure. "But I can't tell you who she is."

"You won't."

"All right, I won't!"

George walked away from him as far as the hollow shadow under the archway, walked his heat and exasperation out of him for a few minutes in the chill of it, and came back to begin all over again. It went on and on and on through the sparse, barren exchange, two, three, four times over; but at the end of it, it was still no. Quivering with tension, exhausted and afraid, Stockwood looked up at him with apprehensive eyes, waiting for the inevitable, and still denied him.

"All right," said George at last, with a sigh, "if that's how you want it, there are more ways than one of finding her."

But were there? Had he discovered even one way yet of finding the man who had picked up Annet and taken her to Birmingham? The city might be, must be, more productive.

"We'll leave it at that," he said, "for the moment. And on your own head be it."

"Are you taking me in?" asked the young man from a dry throat.

"No. Not yet. I don't want you yet, and you'll keep. But you won't do anything rash, will you? Such as deciding to get out of here, fast. I shouldn't. You wouldn't get far."

"I'm not going anywhere," said Stockwood steadily, and sat with his clenched hands braced on his knees, tense and still, as George turned and walked out of the stable block.

Peter Blacklock was waiting in the leaf-strewn border of the drive, just out of sight of the windows of the house.

"Well, did you satisfy yourself?" His kind face was clouded, his eyes anxiously questioning. "You know, Felse, you're barking up the wrong tree. I'm sure Stockwood had nothing whatever to do with it."

"I've finished with him for the time being," said George noncommittally, his voice mild.

"I'm glad. I was sure—"

He fell into step beside George, shaking his head helplessly over his thoughts, and feeling for words.

"You know, Regina and I are very worried about Annet. One can't help realizing, from what was published in the papers, that she's very deeply implicated. What I wanted to say—to ask— You do realize, don't you, that she must have been dragged into this terrible position quite innocently? We know her, you see, very well. It's quite impossible that she should willingly hurt or wrong anyone. She can have known nothing, nothing whatever, about the crime—before or after the act."

He waited, and George walked beside him and said nothing.

"Forgive me, but I had to tell you what we feel about her, we who know her, perhaps, as well as anyone. We're very fond of her, Mr. Felse. I'm sure you can understand that."

"I can understand it," said George. "I'm beginning to think I know her pretty well myself." And could be

very fond of her, too, his mind added, but he kept
that to himself.

"Then you must have realized that she can't have
known anything about murder or theft." He looked
up into George's face with the shadowy, emascu-
lated reflection of his wife's confidence, authority
and energy. "I know this isn't professional conduct,
but I should be very grateful to you for some reassurance—a hint as to how you're thinking of her—"

"I think of her," said George, goaded, "as a human
creature, not a doll, a whole lot more complicated
and dangerous than any of you seem to realize. She
isn't anyone's hapless victim, and she isn't a pawn
in anyone's game, and when I pity her I know I'm
wasting my time. But if it's any consolation to you, I
don't think she's a murderess."

He climbed into the M.G., swung it round, hissing, on the apron of rosy gravel, and drove away
down the avenue of old lime trees, leaving Blacklock
standing with a faint, assuaged smile on his lips and
the deep grief still in his eyes; slender and tall and
elegant in his ancient and excellent clothes, like a
monument to a stratum of society into which he had
been drafted just in time to decay with it.

George telephoned Superintendent Duckett from
home, over the hasty lunch Bunty had spent so much
time and care preparing, and he had now no leisure
to enjoy.

"The bike again," said Duckett hopefully. "If you
can find where they stayed there may be a real
chance of finding out if anyone saw the bike around.
And if so, then it's looking unhealthy for our friend.
But why, for God's sake, say he spent the weekend
with a woman, if he really is the one who was off
with the Beck girl? You'd have thought he'd turn out

absolutely any tale rather than go so near the truth."

"He did, originally. It fell down under him. This time he was pushed. And of course," said George cautiously, "there's always the chance that it may be true—even provably true, if it's that or his neck. He's a good-looking chap, and there could be other women, besides Annet, who'd think so. Even some others he might risk a good deal before he'd name."

"You've got one in mind?" said Duckett alertly, hearing the note of wary thoughtfulness he knew how to interpret.

"I have, but it's farfetched. I'd rather plough other ground first, it's more likely to yield."

He could picture in Technicolor Duckett's face if the receiver should blurt out baldly in his ear: "Well, he *could* have gone off back to Gloucester, and spent the weekend amusing Mrs. Blacklock between lectures and discussions. She's noticed him, all right. She speaks up for him, as well she might if she knows where he was but doesn't want to have to say so—and a little more freely than you would normally for a good chauffeur you'd had only three months, and who otherwise meant nothing to you. And what would be more likely to shut his mouth, and make him stick out even the threat of a murder charge rather than come out with the real facts? A blazing scandal, her reputation gone and his job, and where would he get another in a hurry? If it was Regina, it all makes sense!"

No, that was all true enough, but not for publication, and for the moment nonessential in any case. It couldn't catch their murderer for them, even if they proved it; it could only cancel out one more possibility. The elimination of Stockwood could wait its turn.

"I'm making for Birmingham now," he said, aloud. "It looks the more profitable end at the moment."

"Give 'em my love," said Duckett. "And keep off their corns."

George drove to Birmingham, and conferred with his opposite numbers there briefly and amicably. They had worked together on other occasions, and understood each other very well. Hag-ridden and undermanned, the city C.I.D. were hardly likely to chill their welcome for someone who came with a handful of suggestions, however dubious; all the more if he was willing to investigate them himself.

The sum of their own discoveries, up to then, was two shop assistants who had sold clothing to Annet in one of the big stores, and one elderly newsboy from whom she had bought a paper on Friday evening.

"Never reads the damned things himself," complained the Superintendent bitterly, "except the racing page. Says he's seen too many of 'em to care. Waving the girl's face in front of the rush hour crowds, and never noticed it himself!"

"She was alone when they saw her?"

"Every time."

"Well, let's see if we can get anything out of her old classmates."

The student of literature was out of town for the weekend; he should, of course, have thought of that. But her lodgings were easy enough to find, shared with three other students, and presided over by a competent matron of fifty, who had reared a family of her own, and knew all the pitfalls. It was clear within ten minutes that it would be quite impossible for any irregularities to creep into her well-ordered household, or any of her girls to misbehave herself or entertain a misbehaving visitor within these walls. Contact with Beryl there might have been, but on the whole even that was improbable. The one girl who was spending the weekend in town, over a crucial essay, had never heard Annet mentioned, and never seen her, and from her George gathered that Beryl's time and attention was very largely taken up by men friends rather than women. He wrote that one off, and made for the retired teacher who had enjoyed Annet's liking and confidence.

Miss Roscoe was rosy and gray and garrulous, of uncertain memory, but certain that she had not heard from or seen Annet Beck for over a year.

It took him some time to run the art student to earth, for Myra Gibbons had known no exact address for her, and before he could find her he had to find the secretary of the school. But he had luck, and when at last he located the small old house in a quiet road, and the side door in the yard which led directly to the converted first-floor flatlet, it was Mary Clarkson in person who opened the door to him.

No, she had not seen Annet Beck during the weekend, because she had herself been home in Comerbourne for a whole week, and left the flat closed up. She knew, of course, about Annet's picture being in the paper, and the appeal for information about her, but she had had no information to give. She was terribly concerned about her, of course, but mostly just plain astonished, because it seemed so incredible.

They wrote to each other very occasionally. When had she last written? Oh, maybe a month ago. And had she mentioned that she would be going home for such a long visit at half-term? Yes, she believed she had, now that he came to suggest it. It was terrible about Annet, wasn't it? But no, she'd never told Mary anything about boys, or not about any special boy. Annet didn't confide that kind of thing. No, nothing at all, never a word to indicate that she was either in love or in trouble. She was quite sure. She'd have been curious enough to read between the lines and try to work it out in detail, if ever there'd been the slightest hint.

It appeared that he had drawn a blank again, and the hours of his single and irreplaceable day were slipping away from him with nothing gained. But when she was letting him out, and he looked round the yard and saw how securely enclosed it was, with no window overlooking it, and no other door sharing it, his thumbs pricked.

"Where's the actual door of the house?"

"Oh, that's round the corner in the other street. This was the back door originally, but when she had the flat made to let, she made use of this door to serve it, and walled it off from the kitchen and the passage. That's what makes it so beautifully private."

And so it did, so beautifully private that now he could not be mistaken, and he could not and would not go back with nothing to show for it.

"Has Annet ever been here?"

"Oh, yes, two or three times. She stayed with me once, just overnight, but that's a long time ago."

"She never asked about coming again? Or suggested that she might borrow the flat when you were away?"

"No, not exactly. I mean, *she* didn't. But I remember *I did* tell her, when she was here, that she could make use of it if ever she wanted to be in Birmingham, even if I wasn't here. I told her to ask Mrs. Brookes for the spare key, if she needed it. And I told Mrs. Brookes about it, just in case she came. But she never did—"

She let the ending trail away into silence. She stared at George.

"I think," said George, "we'd better have a word with Mrs. Brookes." He made for the yard door, and the girl came eagerly after, hard on his heels. "When did you get back into town?"

"Only this morning. We haven't got any classes until Monday, but I'm meeting someone tonight, or I should have stayed over until tomorrow evening. I haven't seen her to talk to yet. Do you really think—"

"Yes," said George, and headed round the corner at speed to ring the bell at the coy blue front door. "Were there no signs of occupation?"

"Not that I noticed. Everything was tidy, and just as I left it. But it would be—she was always tidier than I am. And I haven't really looked for anything, why should I? I never even thought of it."

The door was opened, softly and gradually. A thin, small, elderly woman in black, of infinite gentility, glanced enquiringly over George, and smiled in swift, incurious understanding, reassured, at sight of the girl beside him.

"Ah, there you are, my dear," said Mrs. Brookes. "I caught just a glimpse of you this morning when you came in with the shopping, but I thought you'd look in during the day sometime. Your friend was here last weekend—I expect she left a message for you, didn't she? I gave her the key, and she promised she'd leave everything nice for you. Such a pretty child, I was glad to see her again. And no trouble at all," she said serenely, smiling with vague benevolence at the remembered image of Annet, shy, silent and aloof, clenched about her secret. "Quiet as a mouse about the place. And she thanked me so sweetly when she brought the key back on Tuesday evening. If only all the young girls nowadays had

such pretty manners, I'm sure there wouldn't be any
occasion for all this talk about what are the younger
generation coming to."

"She's seventy-one," said George, reporting over an
acrid cup of tea and a Birmingham sausage roll that
represented all the meal he was going to have time
for. "A widow, no relations very close, a few friends,
but they don't pop in at all hours. She's not very
active or strong, her groceries and laundry are
delivered, no dog to walk— Astonishing how completely isolated and insulated you can be in a city, if
you let it happen. And she's the kind that doesn't
mind, not even particularly inquisitive. She doesn't
take a newspaper, except on Sundays, because she
gets all the news the modern way. Where we made
our mistake was bothering about the press at all. It
seems what we should have done was put the girl's
photograph on television. She follows that, all right,
religiously. As it was, she simply didn't know—after
all this labor she really didn't know—what our girl
looked like. Not that she's been able to tell us very
much even now, but at least we know now where
Annet and her boyfriend spent their nights. And
knowing that, it's surely only a matter of time finding
out more. Mrs. Brookes may not be the nosy type,
but there must be somebody in that street who
spends her time peering through the net curtains to
watch everybody's comings and goings. Somebody
will have seen them—some other old girl who doesn't
see the papers, or didn't want to get mixed up in the
business. They still come like that our way, I don't
know about Birmingham."

"They still come like that here, too," the Superintendent assured him grimly, and went on with his
notes.

"Even some old soul too blind to identify a photograph may have a pretty good eye for general appearances, height, walk, the basic cut of a man. The knocking on doors begins now, all along the street. Thank God that's your job, not mine."

"Not mine, either," said the Superintendent with a tight smile, "if I know it. A hate of legwork got me where I am. Check on this for me. The girl came for the key on Thursday evening about seven—by which time it was dark—reminded Mrs. Brookes that her friend had given her permission for her to use the flat any weekend. And Mrs. Brookes remembered and obliged. Girl said she didn't need anything, she had everything, and old lady left her alone to run her own show. The entrance is private, a motorbike could lie in the yard there and not be seen. Old lady saw her three or four times during the weekend, coming home with shopping. Not only food, but fancy bags from a dress shop, very natural in any girl. But always alone. Two or three times they chatted for a few minutes, but that was all. Never saw a man there. Voices don't carry through the walls that I can believe, those are old houses, and solid. No mention of a man, no glimpse of a man, but with her windows facing the opposite way, and her eye on television most of the time, anyhow, that doesn't mean much. Anyhow, she can tell us nothing about a man, and she won't hear of one. Not in connection with this angelic girl. And on Sunday morning Beck was in the local church for morning service, alone, which only reinforces Mrs. Brookes's opinion that we're misjudging her cruelly. On Tuesday evening she brought back the key, said thank you prettily, and left, by what means of transport Mrs. Brookes doesn't know. We could," he said sourly, "have done with a more inquisitive landlady, that's a fact."

"There'll be a neighbor with a flattened nose some- where around. The girls who sold Annet the dress and the nightdress didn't add much, either."

"She shopped alone. Every time. And in city shops and a supermarket, never in the small local places. If he was with her, he waited outside. Most men do. So that's it. That's the lot. But at least we've moved, and now we can keep moving."

"That's the lot. And I've got to be on my way," said George, pushing away his empty cup. "Mrs. Brookes promised me to try and dredge up every word they said to each other, or anything she can remember about the girl. If she does come through with any- thing, call me, will you? I'll give you a ring as soon as I get in at the office, and give you anything new we've got at that end. Not that I expect anything," he said honestly, turning up the collar of his coat in the doorway against the thin wind that had sprung up with dusk. "Yet," he said further, and went round to the parking ground to pick up the car.

He was later than he'd said he'd be, getting back to the office in Comerbourne. Tom Kenyon had tele- phoned once already, with nothing to report but a blameless day of chaotic activity among the geogra- phers, and a continuing watch on the Hallowmount, which would be faithfully maintained until he and his helpers were either called off or relieved. He had promised to ring again in half an hour, which meant he might be on the line again at any moment.

But when the telephone rang again, and George leaned across to pick it up, the voice that boomed in his ear belonged to the Superintendent in Birming- ham.

"Thought you'd be making it about now," he said wit satisfaction. "Two bits of news for you, for what they're worth. First, we've found a small boy who lives three doors away from Mrs. Brookes's back premises, and plays football in the street there. They will do it. He kicked the ball over the wall into Miss Clarkson's yard on Friday morning, and knowing she was away, opened the door and let himself in to fetch it. He says there was a motorbike propped on its stand inside there. A B.S.A. three-fifty. That fits?"

"It fits," said George, aware of a sudden lurch forward, as though he had been astride just such a mount, and accelerating along a closed alley between blank walls. "He didn't, by any chance, collect registrations?"

"No luck, he didn't. Bright as a button about what interests him, he's completely dim about the number. But if it was there, somebody else must have seen it, if we look hard enough. Somebody will have seen the rider, too. It's only a matter of slogging, now we know where to look. And the second thing. Mrs. Brookes has had an afterthought. Don't ask me what it means, or even if it means anything. Myself, I'd be inclined to suppose she made it up to bolster her own picture of the visiting angel, if she didn't in other ways strike me as being scrupulously honest in her observations, if not exactly acute. She says there *was* mention of a man. It didn't occur to her when she was talking to you, because it was so obvious that you were enquiring about someone very different. But she remembered it afterward, and thought she ought to correct her statement, however irrelevant this information may be."

"I recognize," said George, "the style."

"Good, now make sense of the matter. So far, I

can't. She says when Annet Beck fetched the key on Thursday, she told her that she would probably be having a visitor during the weekend. Said he had to be in Birmingham, so he'd be looking in to see her—"

"He?" said George, ears pricked, suddenly aware that this was going to be the place where the cul-de-sac ended, and he must brake now, and hard, if he wanted to keep his head unbroken.

"He. The man for whose presence she was apparently preparing Mrs. Brookes, just in case he should be seen. The only man in the case. And know who she said he'd be? This'll shake you! *Her father!*"

CHAPTER 9

Promptly at five-thirty Tom Kenyon telephoned again.

"Nothing new here. It was a good day out, but nothing whatever happened. I suppose that was exactly what we could expect, with forty-two of us clambering about all over the rocks. If there is anything here to be found, you can stake your life nobody came for it today. But we didn't find it, either."

"Were you able to do any looking?" It wouldn't be easy, with a handful of sharp-eyed juniors on the watch for every eccentricity in their elders.

"Some. Not to attract attention, though, and that means we could only look very superficially at the outcrop areas where the kids were swarming. We had a go at the ring of trees, and the old footways down below, until the boys came down to hunt over the tips for crystals among the calcite. But all we collected was pocketsful of Jane's rock specimens. She always loads them onto the nearest human pack mules to carry home for her. Women know what they're doing, having no pockets."

"They've all come down by this time, I suppose?" said George.

"Ostentatiously. I thought it might be a good idea to leave with as much noise as possible, in case someone somewhere was waiting his turn. But Mallindine and your boy are still up there," he said reassuringly, "keeping an eye on things from cover until I go back. I'm on my way now, I'm going to send them down to get tea here at the pub."

"The others have gone?"

"Yes, into Comerford with their coach, for tea. Jane arranged it. And then home to Comerbourne and disperse. Dead quiet up there now."

He could feel the quietness of the Hallowmount moving, growing, pouring through the dusk toward the village, flowing round and over Fairford and Wastfield, drowning this isolated telephone box on the edge of the wilds. Down the darkening flanks the streams of silence ran softly and slowly, curling round the scattered buildings of the farm, sweeping greenly over the roof of the Sparrowhawk's Nest. All day waiting like a great beast asleep, the long ridge stretched and stirred now in the first chill of twilight, and the little, quivering, treacherous ground wind awoke and began curling its tremulous pathways up through the long grass.

"Can you hold on there until I come out to meet you?"

"Yes, I'll be somewhere on top. I've had tea. I'll send the boys down and wait for you."

"Good! I'll be along as soon as I've talked to the Superintendent. And had a look in at Fairford, perhaps, if you don't mind hanging on another half hour or so?"

"I don't mind. Whenever you can make it, I'll be

here. Don't pass up anything you should do first." He
hesitated, unsure how much right he had to ask
questions but aching with the effort to contain them.
"Did you turn up anything useful at your end?"

"Maybe. Difficult to tell as yet. We've found where
they stayed. Not a hotel—they borrowed a flat rented
by a friend of Annet's. The motorbike appears again.
No one saw the man. But according to the old lady
round the corner, the owner of the house, Annet told
her she was expecting a visitor. Annet described
him to her as her father."

The indrawn breath at the other end of the line
hissed agonizingly, as though the listener had
flinched from a stab wound. "Her *father?*"

"Does that suggest anything?"

It suggested far too much, things Tom had never
wanted to hear, and did not want to remember,
possibilities he could not bear to contemplate. He
choked on exclamations that would unload a share of
the burden onto George's shoulders, bit them back
and swallowed them unuttered. They lay in his
middle like lead.

"It sounds as if we have to revise our ideas, doesn't
it?"

"It does," said Tom, his throat constrained.

"Why say that, unless it was to prepare the way in
case she was seen with this man? A man obviously,
in that case, respectable enough to pass for her
father. *And old enough.*"

"Not a teenager run wild," said Tom.

"Not even a youngster in his twenties. A father
figure. If only just. One could pass for Annet's father
at around forty, maybe, but hardly earlier. Any
ideas?"

The distant voice said hoarsely, aware how little
conviction it must be carrying, "No ideas."

"You be thinking about it," said George, and rang off without more words.

And what did that mean, on top of all the confusions that had bludgeoned him since noon? What was it young Tom Kenyon knew that George didn't know, concerning some man who might be, but was not, Annet's father? And why, feeling as he felt about Annet, and longing as he must long for an end to this uncertainty that held a potential death for her, why had he gulped back his knowledge from the tip of his tongue in panic, and resisted his solid-citizen instinct to plump it into the arms of the police and get rid of the responsibility?

George turned out the lights in the cold office, locked the door after him, and went to make his report in person to Superintendent Duckett. But Annet's father, and Annet's fictional father, and Annet's father's lodger, and the accidental intimacies and involuntary reactions of proximity mingled and danced in his mind all the way.

It was nearly half past six when he reached Fairford. He didn't know why he felt so strongly that he must go there; he had no reason to suppose that anything new had happened there, least of all that Annet would have unsealed her lips and repented of her silence. Nor was he going to try to prise words out of her by revealing any part of what he had found out. That he knew from ample trial to be useless. It was rather that he felt the need to reassure himself that there was still an Annet, a living intelligence, an identity surely not dependent on any other creature for its single and unique life, a girl who could still be saved. Because if she was past saving, the main object of this pursuit was already lost. The old dead man had his rights to justice, but the young living girl was the more urgent charge now upon George's heart.

He turned in at the overgrown gate, into the darkness of the untrimmed, autumnal trees, the soft rot of leaves like wet sponge under his wheels. He came out of the tunnel of shadow, and sudden lances of light struck at his eyes. The front door stood wide open, all the lights in the house were blazing, the curtains undrawn. In the shrubberies down toward the brook someone was threshing about violently. In the garden, somewhere behind the house, someone was bleating frantically like a bereaved ewe, and until George had stopped the engine and scrambled out of the car he could not distinguish either the voice or the words. Then it sprang at him clearly, and he turned and ran for the house.

"Annet! Annet!" bellowed Beck despairingly, crashing through the bushes.

George bounded up the steps and into the hall, and Policewoman Lilian Crowther leaned out of the living room doorway with the telephone receiver at her ear, and dropped it at sight of him, and gasped, "Thank God! I was trying to get through to you. She's gone!"

"When?" He caught at the swinging telephone and slammed it back on its rest, seized the girl by the arm and drew her with him into the room. "Quick! When? How long ago?"

"Not more than five minutes. We found out a few minutes ago. Lockyer's out there looking for her—and her father. She can't be far."

"You shouldn't have left her."

"She collapsed! Like that other time. She was lying with her head nearly in the hearth, and I couldn't lift her alone. I ran for her mother to help me—"

The window was wide open, the curtains swinging in the rising wind of the evening. Mrs. Beck blundered past through the shaft of light, running with aimless urgency, turning again to run the other way, her face contorted into a grimace of weeping, but without tears or sound. As though death was all round the house, just outside the area of light, and everyone had known and recognized it except Annet; as though she was lost utterly as soon as she broke free from the circle and ran after her desire, and none of them would ever see her again. As though, plunging out of the window, she had plunged out of the world.

George vaulted the sill and landed on the edge of the unkempt grass. Mrs. Beck turned and stared at him with dazed eyes, and caught at his arm.

"She's gone! I couldn't help it, no one could stop her if she was so set to go. It isn't anyone's fault. What could we do?"

"I'm not blaming you," he said, and put her off, and ran through the trees to the boundary fence, leaving her stumbling after him. No moon, but even in the starlight of half a sky the emptiness about Fairford showed sterile and motionless. He had met no girl on the road. She would keep to the trees as long as she could. He circled the grounds hurriedly, halting now and again to freeze and listen. He heard Beck baying at the remotest edge of the garden, and met Lockyer methodically threading the shrubberies.

"No sign of her?"

"No sign, sir. I heard your car. Crowther'll have told you—"

"Keep looking," said George, and turned back at a

run toward the house. He overtook Mrs. Beck on the way, and drew her in with him.

"Here, sit down by the fire and be quiet. Lilian, close the window and get her a drink." He shut the door with a slam, and leaned his back against it. "Now, what happened?"

"I told you, she collapsed, she almost fell into the fire. How could I know it was a fake? I ran for Mrs. Beck—she was upstairs, she didn't hear me call. When we came back Annet was gone."

"She climbed out of the window," said Mrs. Beck, hugging her writhing hands together in her lap to keep them still. "Without even a coat—in her thin house shoes!"

"Yes, yes, I know all that." And Lockyer, patrolling dutifully outside, couldn't be on every side of the house at once. Annet could move like a cat; she hadn't found it difficult to elude him on her own ground. "But before! Something happened, something gave her the word. Why tonight? Why now? She chose her time, she had a reason. Has she had any letters? Telephone messages?"

"No," said Lilian Crowther positively. "I've been with her all the time until she dropped like that. And Mrs. Beck reads her letters—but anyhow there haven't been today."

"And no visitors," said George, fretting at his own helplessness, and caught the rapid flicker of a glance that passed uneasily between them. "No visitors? Someone *has* been here?"

"I asked him to come," said Mrs. Beck loudly. "I asked him to talk to her and do what he could. What else is he for, if not to help people in trouble? I thought he might get something out of her. It was last night being choir practice that made me think of it. I telephoned him and asked him to come in today.

There couldn't be any harm in that. If she couldn't see her own vicar—even criminals are allowed that."

"All right," said George, frantically groping forward along this unforeseen path, "so the vicar came. No one else?"

"No one else. You must admit I had the right—"

"All right, you had the right! Was he left alone with her?"

"No," said Lilian, defensively and eagerly, "I was with her all the time. Mrs. Beck left them together, but I stayed in the room."

"Thank God for that! Annet didn't object?"

"She didn't seem to care one way or the other."

And yet she had bided her time, and torn herself resolutely out of their hold. Something had passed, something significant. Why other wise should she have chosen this particular hour, after waiting so long and so stoically? "Well, what did they have to say to each other? Everything you can remember."

She dredged up a number of embarrassed, agonizing platitudes through which the adolescent rawness of pity showed like flesh through torn clothing. The vicar was back in the room with them, convulsed with sympathy and hideously unable to contain it, or spill it, or wring his inadequate if kindly heart open and give it to her frankly; an aging boy with only a boy's heaven to offer anyone, and stunted angels with undeveloped wings like his own.

"He said he was to tell her the choir had missed her at practice, and sent her their prayers. He said they took comfort in the thought that they would meet her at six-thirty at the altar. If only in the spirit, he said. And that was about all," she concluded lamely, scouring her memory in vain for more vital matter. "It doesn't seem anything to set her off like this."

And yet she had received, somehow, the summons that sent her out into the dusk. He could not be mistaken. If it was not here, in this trite comfort, then there must be something else, something they had missed.

"Nothing else happened? He didn't give her a note from someone else?"

"No, honestly. He never went near enough to hand her anything. You'd have thought he was afraid of her—I suppose he was, in a way," said Policewoman Crowther, with more perception than George would have given her credit for.

"She didn't see the paper?" He hadn't seen it himself; he didn't know if there was anything in it to speak to her, but somewhere the lost thread dangled, and must be found again.

"No, she never tried to. She never showed any interest."

Perhaps, thought George, because she knew they wouldn't let her have the papers even if she wanted them. Perhaps because she had waited with such fatal confidence for the only message she needed, and knew it would not come that way.

But then there was nothing left but those few, bald sentences, brought from the outside world by the vicar; and if the clue was nowhere else, it must be there. The choir had missed her—Mrs. Beck must have telephoned him just before he went over to the church for practice, and he had unburdened his heart to her colleagues to spread the load. And nobly they had responded. Or had they? The tone of the message was surely his, or a careful parody. It sounded as though he had dictated, and they had said: Amen. They sent her their prayers. They would meet her at six-thirty at the altar. If only in the spirit. Six-thirty was the hour of evensong, that was plain enough. Yes, but it belonged to tomorrow, not today. Why did it send her out tonight. George sweated through it word by word, and darkness, rather than light, fell on him in the moment of discovery, stunning him.

Six-thirty at the altar. Six-thirty at the Altar! All the difference in the world.

Six-thirty!

Twenty to seven by his watch, and she was somewhere out there in the dark, with a quarter of an hour's start of him at least, bursting her heart on the steep climb to her lover.

He tore the door open and was out of it and down the steps in a couple of raking strides, before they realized that he had found what he was looking for. Racing toward his car, he shouted peremptorily for Lockyer, and by the time he had the M.G. turned recklessly in the confined space and pointing down the drive, the bushes threshed before the constable's galloping body, and Lockyer was running beside him. George slowed, and shoved open the door.

"Get in, quick! Never mind searching, you're not needed here. I know now where to look."

Lockyer fell lurching into the seat beside him, and slammed the door. They rocked out through the gate and swung left into the narrow road.

"Where are we going?" Lockyer clung to the dashboard, and hefted his big body to speed the turn, panting after his run.

"Top of the Hallowmount."

"For God's sake, what's she doing rushing up there?"

"Meeting her lover. He sent for her."

Her lover, if he still was that, after being hunted for days, and nursing for days the knowledge that the case against him depended entirely upon her. More likely by now it was her murderer she was going to meet. One can run faster and live more cheaply than two, hide more easily, remain anonymous more surely. And besides, the bulk of the evidence would die with Annet. Even when he made up his mind to run, he couldn't, he daren't, run until he had silenced her. God alone knew what she thought they were going to do. Run away together, maybe, to the ends of the earth, ditch the B.S.A. somewhere, hitch lifts, reach the sea and the chance of a passage over to France.

Maybe! Or maybe she had something else in mind, something passionate and individual and her own, not to be guessed at too confidently by anyone in the world; because no one in the world knew Annet well enough to be sure what she would do, but George Felse by this time knew her at least well enough to wait with humility, and wonder, and acknowledge that she was a mystery.

Past the Wastfield gate, bounding and wallowing over the cart ruts, and on between the rough pastures, fence posts blurring into a continuous flickering wall of pallor alongside. Half the sky dark over them, but glimmerings of starlight still. Pale objects shone lambent out of the darkness, a tall gate post where the plantation began, the wall of a barn in the field opposite. Before them the Hallowmount loomed, cutting off the dapplings of the sky, its great bulk languid but aware.

"But *how* did he get word to her? Or was it all arranged between them before?"

All arranged, maybe, though they'd expected to make their bid for freedom in other circumstances than these. All arranged but the time and the place, perhaps even the place accepted, established by old usage. And the time he had appointed, and she was keeping her appointment. Without even a coat. In her thin house shoes.

"Her visitor brought the message this afternoon."

"Her visitor? But there wasn't anybody, except—"

Members of the clergy, like doctors and postmen, tend to be invisible, but that big, comely, well-meaning figure sprang into sharp focus now, became male, personable and possible in Lockyer's eyes. He swallowed, appalled. "What, the *vicar?*" He swallowed again, swallowed voice and all, and sat stunned.

Her father! Well, he was old enough to fill the bill, if only just old enough, he made sense of the description; and nobody had enquired into his movements. Why should they? Certainly he was at choir practice, that night when Annet missed it, certainly he was at church and fulfilling his usual duties on the Sunday. But a man can be in Comerford church at half past seven, and in Birmingham by nine o'clock, or shortly after. One man had.

"But—the *vicar!*" persisted Lockyer, gulping dismay and disbelief.

George said nothing to that; he was busy holding the car steady over the worst patch of road without slackening speed. He knew now. This time he couldn't be wrong, and he wasn't in any cul-de-sac, with a blank wall at the end of it waiting for him to crash at speed.

He saw the rough grasses of the slope put on form behind the wire fence, the crouching bulk of the hill withdraw into its true dimension. He brought the car around into the arc of short grass by the second plantation gate, and scrambled out of the driver's

door and through the wires of the fence with Lockyer pounding at his back. Head down, lungs pump-
ing, he breasted the first slope, got his rhythm, and
began to climb the Hallowmount faster than he had
ever climbed a hill in his life.

Tom Kenyon sat in a niche of the rocks on the
highest point of the Altar, and stared along the
ridge. It was the first time he had ever been up here
alone, and the strangest thing to him was that it did
not feel like the first time. The silence that had
flowed down into the valleys with the dropping
twilight was absolute now; it lay like a cloak over
the whole great, wakeful shape of rock and pasture,
smoothed and molded to the stretched body. Sometimes he felt a rhythm stirring under him, like deep
and easy breathing, and found himself tuning his
own breath to the same measure. Sometimes he fell,
without realizing it, into such a stillness that the
faintly seen shapes of his own circling arms and
clasped knees seemed to have acquired the texture
and solidity of rock, as though he had grown into the
quartzite of the Altar. He had no sense of undergoing
a new experience; this was rather a recollection,
drawn from so deep within him that he felt no desire
to explore its origins, for that would have been
dissecting his own identity, or to question its valid-
ity, for that would have been to doubt his own. He
felt the tension of long ages of human habitation
drawing him into the ground, absorbing him, making
him part of the same continuity.

Miles had been right; fear was inappropriate and
irrelevant. Awe remained with him, and grew, but
not fear. And if Miles had been right about that, too,
then belonging was all. It could happen to you

without any motion on your part. Suddenly it was, and you were in it. You belonged, you respected, you partook, you contributed, this earth and all its layers of ancestral bones accepted you; a better and safer, a more impregnable security than belonging to a tribe or conforming to a society could give you.

How strange that you should have to clamber alone into some remote, wild place like this, into this articulate silence and this teeming solitude, to discover where you came from and where you were going, and in what company. I belong, therefore I am.

The ground wind had dropped, the grasses were motionless. The cold, clear air hung still. He heard, with some detached sense that did not suffer his deeper silence to be broken, light, distant sounds from the edges of Comerford, the faint, far hum of cars on country roads, a motorcycle climbing steadily, small synthetic echoes from other worlds.

And all this time, side by side with this unbelievable serenity of mind, the horror possessed him that had fallen upon him when George Felse had said: "Annet described him as her father."

There was nothing new to be thought or felt about it now, but he could not let it rest, his mind trod round and round the same path endlessly, agonized and finding no reassurance.

George had taken it to mean merely that she was preparing the way for some man respectable enough and old enough to pass for her father, in case they should be seen together. But supposing she had been using the term more precisely than that? Supposing she really meant the man everyone thought of as her father?

He had tried to get the idea out of his mind, but it would not leave him. All the details that might have

presented discrepancies, and delivered him from
the nightmare, came treacherously and fell into
place. Beck had been home all the weekend? Oh, no,
by his own account and his wife's, he hadn't. He'd
tramped the lanes and the streets of Comerford most
of Thursday night, but after that he'd gone off by bus
to his sister's place at Ledbury and his cousin's
smallholding in the Teme valley, in case Annet had
turned up there. He'd come home only on Monday
night. Nobody had checked his statements, why
should they? Not even his wife. Nobody knew that
he wasn't really Annet's father, nobody except Mrs.
Beck and Tom Kenyon.

Unless Annet knew. That was the whole point. *Did
Annet know?* And if so, how long had she known? He
pondered that painfully, and he could not avoid the
fear that she did know it, and had known it for a long
time. It accounted all too reasonably for her inac-
cessibility, her estrangement from them both. From
Beck as father, that is. But Beck as a man?

Was it too farfetched? It would be an appalling
tragedy, but it could happen. There was an even
worse thought peering at him relentlessly from the
back of his mind: that Beck had told her the truth
himself, because he could not feel toward her as his
daughter, knowing she was not, and his sick conscience would not let him rest until he had made
confession. He was a stickler for truth and duty in
his ineffective way; he might even have meant it for
the best.

And she—how could you ever be sure about Annet? She might have reacted with warmth and indignation and tenderness, from which the slippery path
to love is not so far. And granted that as a possibility,
into what a desperate and piteous situation they had
trapped each other. Flight, robbery, murder might

well come to look like legitimate ways out of it, if no other offered.

He wished now that he had told George, he even made strenuous resolutions to tell him as soon as he came; but in his heart he knew that he never would. He could not repeat what he had heard from an overwrought and drunken man; he had no right to break that lamentable confidence.

As often as he reached the end of this reappraisal, and turned to look at the whole idea with a more critical eye, he was convinced that he was mad, that it was impossible, that he had a warped mind; but as soon as he began a feverish examination of the details, in the hope of throwing it out altogether, he knew that it could happen, that such things had happened, that there was no immunity from the abnormal even in a world of careful normality, and no place to hide from love if it came for you. Look at his own case! Had he ever wanted to love her? Does anybody ever want to walk into the fire?

Half past six by his watch. The small, luminous pinpoints of the figures were the only brightness in this calm, immemorial, secret dark. He stirred, finding his limbs cramped by the gathering chill, and slid down from his perch into the grass. George would surely be here soon. And almost inevitably the two boys, though told to go home after their tea, would use their own obstinate judgment, and come back to share what was left of his vigil. More than likely even Jane, having packed her coach load off to Comerbourne in charge of a couple of prefects, would return to see how he had fared. It couldn't be long now.

He would be sorry, almost, to have his solitude shared by the living. For all the innumerable gener-ations of the dead, dwindling far into time past,

before the Romans came mining for lead, before the
Iron Age fort on Cleave was dug, before the chipped
flints of Middlehope were made, he had no need of
speech in order to communicate, no need to exert
himself in explanations or response. He was at one
with them without effort of any kind, without rites,
without ritual.

Regina was surely right. There were not, there
never had been, any witches on the Hallowmount.
They would have been inappropriate, derisory, re-
dundant, alien, false. Incantations were for outsid-
ers.

He thought, I'm going queer from being alone,
getting fanciful; there's a twentieth century somewhere around, and we're in trouble in the middle of
it, and no way out that I can see.

And it was then that the small sound that had been
hammering for some minutes at his senses, unnoticed,
achieved actual presence, and made itself known to
him. Time came back with it, and stress, and the
inescapable memory of Annet, mute in the heart of
her pathetic dream of happiness, with wreckage all
round her. He moved out of the enclosing ring of the
rocks, to hear more clearly.

Busy, regular, persistent, the hum of an engine
climbing steadily, not on the Fairford side of the hill,
but down there in the highest reaches of Middlehope. From the western flanks of the Hallowmount
the sound would be cut off completely; here on the
crest he heard it plainly. And when he moved out of
the edge of the slope, looking down over the shallow
bowl of the valley head, he saw the small glowworm
of a headlight weaving its way up by the sheep path
from Abbot's Bale. Light and sound drew steadily
nearer, crossing the boggy patches with assurance,
mounting into the dry pasture where the path van-

ished like a smoke trail on a pale sky. Close beneath
the Altar, in the throat of Middlehope, the motorcycle halted, and in a moment the engine stopped.

   Like a cloud of birds disturbed, the silence
wheeled, circled and settled again. The tiny light
went out. A small, dark figure detached itself from
its mount, and began to climb the slope.

CHAPTER 10

He drew back hurriedly into the circle of rocks about the Altar, the beat of his heart suddenly violent against his ribs, the tatters of time past shuddering away from him. The grating of stones under his own feet sounded like an avalanche to him. He felt with stretched toes for the silent patches of short turf, groped his way round bony elbows of rock into a deep niche of darkness, braced his feet firmly in grass, and took hold on the harsh faces of spar with cautious fingers. With his head drawn back into cover, his cheek against the stone, he could watch the faint, lambent spaces of sky between the outcrops, overhanging the descent into Middlehope. If he failed to see where the intruder emerged, he would surely hear him come.

A motorbike, and a solitary rider climbing purposefully toward this unlikely place in the night! They had not been so far out in their guesses, they had not wasted their day. And here was he alone, not empowered or equipped to do more than observe and identify. Above all identify. That he must do, at whatever cost. Because this could not be coincidence, it could not be innocent. The man climbing the hill was Jacob Worrall's murderer.

How many minutes to mount from the last faint smear of the path above the brook? The head of the valley was shallow and bare, it could not take long. He waited with breath held, but the thudding of blood in his own ears deafened him to more distant sounds, or else there was no rising current of air to lift to this place sounds from too close below. Minutes dripped by like the slow drops of sweat trickling between his shoulder blades, and still nothing. He began to think the newcomer must have swung away from the Altar to traverse toward the trees.

Then he caught the sudden rattle of a stone rolling under a foot, and the grunt of a sharply drawn breath, both startlingly close. He shrank and froze in his cranny, cheek turned painfully against the rock, eyes on the paler levels where sky and earth met.

A head and shoulders, stooped into the effort of climbing, and all but shapeless in consequence, heaved from the dead black on the earth and hunched into the dim blue-black of sky. In lunging strides the shadow lengthened, came over the rim panting with exertion, and straightened and stretched with a sigh of relief as it stepped onto level ground. Against the sky he was a long silhouette, against the rocks, as he came forward, he was shapeless movement, almost invisible, and rapid movement at that. He knew exactly where he was going, and felt no doubt of his solitude.

Tom heard the slur of his steps along the short grass, the deep, whistling breaths he drew, still panting with the exertion of his climb. He was moving diagonally across the space within the rocks, some-

what away from where Tom lay in hiding. Sounds
rather than vision traced his passage, and it was
straight as an arrow to the furrowed faces of spar at
the base of the Altar.

Craning out of his hiding place, straining vision
and hearing after identity, Tom gathered every detail only to doubt it the next moment, where so much
was guessed at blindly. Now the shadow shrank,
dropped together. He heard the effortful subdued
movements that did not belong, surely, to the very
young. And that fitted, now that the woman in
Birmingham had given them the clue. The man was
on his knees, close against the piled boulders of the
outcrop, the buttresses of the Altar. Huddled, head-
less, the dull shadow hunched forward, reaching
with both arms into a crevice of the rock face. The
labored breathing steadied cautiously, the faint sob
at the end of every inhalation swung like a pendulum.

The sound of cautious groping, and a whispered
curse, and then a strong and certain sound, the
grating of stone against stone, as though a heavy
stopper was being withdrawn carefully from the
unglazed neck of a stoneware bottle. The stooping
shoulders heaved back, the bent head reappeared.
Something was laid aside on the grass with a soft
thud, and he leaned and groped forward again, and
again drew back with full hands. A deep sigh of
thankfulness. He turned on his knees to face away
from the rock, and held his prize before him on the
grass.

Tom's heart repeated vehemently and certainly.
Not Beck! Not because of the motorbike. Beck had
never openly owned such a thing, true, but motor-
bikes can be hired, or if necessary bought and kept
secretly. And however grotesque it might seem to

associate Beck's narrow, unworldly nature and mild scholarship with such things, the fact remained that many even odder and more unlikely characters rode them. Not Beck, when it came down to it, only because he so desperately desired that it should not be Beck. But he clung to his certainty, and would not be dislodged from it.

A glowworm of light sprang up abruptly between the arched body and the circling rocks, trained upon the grass. By the tiny pool of pallor it made, it could be only one of those thin pencil flashlights that clip in a breast pocket, and even so the kneeling man held it shrouded in his hand, for his fingers were dimly outlined with the rose-colored radiance of his blood. He could not risk showing a light openly on top of the Hallowmount, but neither could he handle his prize, it seemed, without using the flashlight for a moment or two.

Sharp in the gleam sprang the black outline of a small leather briefcase. He held it flat and steady with a knee, the flashlight cupped over it closely, while with his free hand he turned a key in the lock, tipped the case upright, peered and fumbled within. He had to satisfy himself that his treasure was intact, it represented his funds, his hope of escape, the only future he had. He wanted two hands to manipulate it, and leaned aside for an instant to wedge his flashlight in a crevice low in the rocks, turned carefully on the briefcase and shaded by his draped handkerchief. Now if only he would turn his head, if only the wind would rise and whisk the handkerchief away, so that the shrouded thread of light could expand and reach his face. But the air hung still, charged with indifference and silence.

Turning back feverishly to the examination of the contents of the case, he set his knee astray on the sharp edge of the flat plug of stone he had drawn from the crevice, and winced and gasped, but neither the hissing indrawn breath nor the painful exhalation had any voice to identify him. That cavity within the rocks must have been known to them for a long time, served them as letter box and safe deposit on more than one occasion, but it had surely never had to guard two thousand pounds worth of small jewelry before. Could so small a case hold all that value in jewelry? Tom supposed it could. Most of it had been in good rings; and diamonds and sapphires and a few gold watches will lie in a very little space.

And it seemed there had been room left in the case for something else, besides the stolen jewelry. The motion of the hurrying hands brought it halfway out into the light, the right hand gripped it momentarily with a convulsive clasp, the shape of the hold defining it clearly, even before Tom's straining eyes caught the short black thrust of the barrel.

A tiny thing, a compact handful. Some small-caliber pistol. He knew nothing about guns, he had never handled one. Sometime, somewhere, this man had; the hand knew the motions, though it performed them as in a momentary and terrifying absence of mind. Men of an age to pass for Annet's father had almost all of them been in uniform during the last war, and the trained hands don't forget. And plenty of them had brought home guns at the end of it, and never bothered to hand them in, even after police appeals.

He was satisfied now; he sat back on his heels with a sigh, and thrust the gun down again into the case. His hand was swallowed to the wrist when the sudden sound came, lifted over the crest between them on a random current of air from the

west, from the Fairford side of the ridge. Somewhere below there it might have been fretting at the
edges of their consciousness for a minute or more,
and they had been too intent to notice it; for now it
was startlingly near and clear and resolute, for all its
quietness, the soft slurring of light feet in the grass,
running, stumbling, slipping, recovering, hurrying
uphill to the Altar.

The kneeling man heard it, and wrenched round
frantically to face it, plucking the gun from the
discarded briefcase and bracing it before his body.
His lunging shoulder swept the handkerchief aside
and dislodged the flashlight after it; it fell and rolled
sparkling along the ground, and he leaned after it
with a hoarse gasp and snapped it off into darkness.
But for an instant it had illuminated his tense and
frightened face as it fell.

Tom clung shaking in his niche, the blurred oval of
light and fear still dancing on the darkness before
his eyes. Not Beck! No! Not any of the young bloods
who gathered on the corner of the square in Comerbourne to compare the noisy and ill-ridden mounts
that were their pathetic status symbols. Not young
Stockwood. Not some mercifully expendable stranger.
But Peter Blacklock, estate manager and husband
to the wealthiest woman in West Midshire, secretary of half a dozen worthy bodies that operated
under her shadow, choirmaster, organist, general
factotum of the village, the prince consort of Cwm
Hall.

With the face everything fell into proportion, coher-
ence and certainty, instantly, before the whorls of
light had ceased to float in front of him in the darkness, and long before he relaxed the half-hysterical
grip of his abraded fingertips on the rocks.

Her father! Yes, he would do for that; she could have produced him before Mrs. Brookes without a qualm. Forty-four or so, pleasant and charmingly spoken, mild, easy-humored, with a twist of rueful fun in him, and an uncle to her in her parents' eyes—who could have filled the bill better? And he made sense of so much more than that, by the qualities he had not, by the voids he offered for her to fill. He was as inevitable as he was impossible.

Who else had been in such close contact with her? Thrown together by the hour, casually and practically, in Regina's house, forced together by Regina's pitiless committee work, those two, being what they were, might easily fall together into the abyss of love, and drown, and die. It wasn't as if you were offered a choice. The time might well come when they could not bear it any longer, when they had to escape, had to be together somewhere out of her shadow. And once tasted, how could they let that desperate ecstasy go? Even the opportunist robbery, which at first seemed so improbable in one who had everything, fell implacably into place. *Because he was penniless!*

It was staggering, but it was true. What did he have of his own? From the time he'd married Regina her estates had taken up all his time. And what did he want with a profession when she would gladly buy him or give him anything he wanted? Except, of course, the one thing he had wanted to death, and couldn't ask her for. For that he'd had to provide himself.

Poor devil!

All this passed through Tom's mind by fitful glimpses, like light from a guttering candle, in the few seconds while he listened to the fervent footsteps his heart recognized now only too well. He wanted to call out to her to go back, while there was time, but he'd hesitated too long, and it was too late. Annet was there against the sky, her hair streaming.

Blacklock had lowered the gun; he knew her now, and sprang with open arms to meet her. But the true impetus that flung them together, strained breast to breast in a ravenous embrace, was hers, and had always been hers. She wasn't his victim; he was hers. She had destroyed him by loving him. If she'd never even noticed him, except as a middle-aged man, a father figure, he'd have mastered his feelings for her. But she'd opened to him, she'd loved him, he'd been forced to turn longing and dream into action. No, Annet was nobody's victim, she had done what she had chosen to do, taken him because he was the weakest, the most helpless, the least effective, the unhappiest of all the men it might have been. All good reasons, and there was no going back on them now.

Blacklock said, "Annet!" as a man dying of thirst might have said, "Water!" He had his arms locked round her, the gun, still in his hand, pressed against her back. And then there was a silence that tore at Tom's senses, while they kissed and he burned.

"I thought you weren't coming. I was afraid!"

"I came as soon as I could. You knew I'd come." And again the silence, aching and hurried and brief. "Darling! Darling!" Her deep voice throaty and charged with agonizing tenderness, the implications in its tones of stroking hands, and the deliberate, assuaging pressure of her body, reassuring, caressing, protecting.

"Yes, I knew! If you could, I knew you'd come. But I was afraid. We've got to hurry," he said urgently. "The bike's down below. If we can get an hour's start

we can shake them. They won't look for us westward. And from Ireland—"

He broke off there to take her in more exactly.
"You haven't even got a coat! We must buy you one
somewhere tomorrow. You can wear my windjacket
for tonight." He stooped to snatch up the briefcase
from the ground, and caught Annet by the wrist.
"Come on, hurry, they'll be after us soon."

They would go, he would tow her down the hill in
his wake and drag her into his crime, she who had
done nothing criminal yet. It was more than Tom
could bear. She must not do it. She must not make
herself an accessory after the fact, an outlaw and a
felon, not even for love's sake. To hold her back from
that was something worth dying for.

He didn't know what he was going to do until he
had done it. Scrambling, shouting, he broke out of
the shadow of the rocks and flung himself between
them and the edge of the slope.

"Annet, don't! Don't listen to him! Don't go with
him! Don't make yourself a murderess! Don't—"

Blacklock uttered a soft, terrified cry of panic and
despair, and loosed Annet's arm. Hugging the briefcase to him, he fired blindly at the half-seen figure
that distorted the darkness, fired rather at the
shouting and the threat than at any corporeal oppo-
nent. The impact of the bullet sent Tom staggering
backwards, and swung him partially round before he
dropped.

He groped along the ground, astonished, lucid and
without pain for an instant, dazed by the whirling of
stars over him, and the chill and shock of the ground
under him. Then the pain came, knifing at his
shoulder a full second after the impact, and he cried
out in bitter indignation, one brief, angry shout of
agony. The earth and the sky stilled; he knew him-

self lying at Annet's feet, and felt the stillness of horror holding her paralyzed over him. Fumbling at his left shoulder, he felt the hot stickiness of blood; and when he tried to lift himself on one elbow, he fell back ignominiously into the grass.

Darkness lurched at him, withdrew, stooped again. He fought it off, straining upward obstinately toward Annet's unseen face and frozen stillness.

"Don't go! Don't let him make you." His own voice sounded grotesquely faint and far, and faded like a weak radio signal. He thought he had uttered more words than he heard, and some had been lost, but he went on trying. It was all he could do for her now. "You didn't kill anyone—you didn't steal— Don't let him make you what he is."

There was no way to silence him but one. Shaking, sweating and half blinded, Blacklock passed his forearm across his eyes to clear them, and reached the hand that clutched the briefcase to push Annet out of the way.

"Annet, go on ahead!"

He pointed the gun carefully at the patch of muted darkness heaving on the ground. His finger tightened convulsively on the trigger. The voice *had* to stop. It was like a barrier between them and freedom, there was no escape until it was silenced.

She woke to realization and awareness, starting out of her daze of horror.

"No, don't!" She flung herself between them with arms spread.

"Annet, please!" He dropped the briefcase then to grasp her by the arm and pluck her out of the way, his voice a wail of despair.

Annet tore herself out of his grip and dropped like a bird, stretching her body upon Tom's on the ground, winding her arms about him fiercely. Her cheek was pressed against his, her hair spread silken and cool over his forehead and eyes. Breast to breast, her chin upon his shoulder, she clung to him tenaciously with all her slight, warm, dear weight, covering him from harm.

"*Annet!*"

"No, you shan't, I won't let you!"

And she felt nothing for him, nothing at all! That was worse than the drain of blood out of his burning shoulder, worse than the terror of death. She felt nothing for him, all her agony and resolution was to save her darling from damning himself beneath a still greater load of guilt, a second and more deliberate murder.

Faint and sick, Tom lay quaking with his new knowledge of her. She had never needed him to show her her duty. He should have known it. She had run up here to her meeting without even a coat, without so much as a handkerchief by way of luggage. *She never meant to go!* It was for something quite different she came. And all he had done, with his interference and his disastrous want of understanding, was at best to subject himself to her humiliating pity, and at worst to destroy himself. Live or die, this was the only way he would ever have her arms round him.

He braced his one good hand feebly against her shoulder and tried to push her away from him, outraged by this admission to her mercy while he was excluded from her heart. Light as she was, she clung and would not be dislodged. He was too weak to lift her weight from him. He could not even break her hold. He felt the tears burst from his closed eyelids and dew her cheek, but she did not seem to be aware of them, and he could not even turn his head aside and spare her his humiliation and distress. There was no help for it; he had to submit, he had to hear them fight out their last conflict over his body.

"Get up, Annet! There's no time—" Blacklock was all but weeping.

"No! You shan't touch him, I won't let you. Not again!"

"Let him live, then, I don't care! Anything, whatever you want, only come, quickly! Get up—I won't hurt him, I won't touch him. Only come on, we've only got a few hours at the most."

She unwound her arms from Tom very gently and carefully, and rose from the ground. She kept her body between the wounded man and the gun still, her hands spread on the air, ready to turn and cover him again at the first false word or gesture. Slowly she drew herself upright, and faced her lover.

Low and clearly, "No," she said, "I'm not coming."

He could not believe it. He stared, the gun drooping and trembling in his hand. *"Annet!"*

"Peter, don't go! Come back with me, it's the only way. Come back and face them. Oh, why *did you? Why did you?* There wasn't anything I wanted, except you. Surely you knew that? And now there's nothing we can do except go back together. Can't you see that?"

He repeated, *"Annet!"* whimpering, unable to understand but already transfixed with terror.

"I'll stay with you, don't be afraid." She went toward him, her hands out to touch him, and he gave back before her as though she had been an advancing fire. "As long as they let me, I'll stay with you. I won't forsake you. Only don't run, and hide, and kill again. You'd have to, once you began running. Stop now! *That poor old man!*" she said, and her voice was a soft, dreadful cry of pain. "Come back with me and give yourself up. Darling, darling, trust me and come! I can't bear the other way for you, it's too horrible."

He couldn't believe it. He drew breath, sobbing, fumbling toward her and starting away again. "You must come! You said you'd come! Oh, God! Oh, God! Annet, you can't abandon me!" No louder than the stirring of the breeze that came so late, his voice wept and raged, and Tom could not stop hearing it.

"I'm not abandoning you, I'm here with you. As long as they let me I shall be with you. Always, everywhere. But I won't go away with you. What we've done we've done, we have to stand to it now. Come back with me!"

Helpless under their feet, the blood draining steadily out of him into the ground, Tom shut eyes and ears and willed his senses to withdraw from them and leave him darkened and out of reach. But there was no escape. He tried to turn on his face, clawing at the ground with his one good hand, struggling to drag himself away by the fistfuls of long grass that brushed cold along his cheek; but he could move only by inches, and there was no place to hide.

Where was his conception of love now, beside this tormented passion? They had forgotten him. For each of them no one existed but the other; he pleading with her to escape with him, refusing to go without her, refusing as desperately to turn and go back with her; she absolute and inflexible to save him from further evil, begging him, willing him to turn and walk of his own volition toward his expiation and salvation.

"You want me taken! You want them to hang me!"

"You know I don't. I want you intact, I want you free. There isn't any virtue unless you choose it freely."

How could he choose it? He was too feeble and too afraid.

"You don't love me," he moaned, helpless to go or stay.

"It's *because* I love you!"

"Then you've got to come with me. You *shall* come with me," he said in a broken howl of despair, "or I'll kill you. I'd rather that than leave you behind."

"Yes!" Incredibly she seized on that as the answer to her deepest anxiety. Her voice lifted into joy, her broken movements toward her lover took fire in a sudden blaze of confidence and eagerness. "Yes, kill me! That would be best. Kill me! I want you to."

She had taken two soft, rapid paces toward him, she had him by the hand that held the gun, and was raising it softly, softly, toward her breast, with infinite care not to startle or frighten him. Her long fingers gentled his wrist, encircling and caressing him.

"Yes, kill me, Peter. I mean it. Then I'll be there waiting for you, and you won't be alone or afraid. Don't be afraid of anything. I won't forsake you. I love you! Kill me!"

Passionate, persuasive and sincere, the voice insisted. Dominant and assured, the hand lifted and guided his hand. Oh, God, oh, God, she really did mean it! There was nothing she would not do for him, dying was not even the ultimate gift she was offering him; she had the hereafter in the other hand, patient companionship through purgatory, half his guilt on her shoulders, and no deliverance for her until he was delivered.

Tom rolled over on his face, and braced his good arm under him to prise himself up from the ground. He had to get to them, there was nobody else. He shouted, or thought he shouted, but they seemed to hear nothing. Red-hot tongs gripped his left shoulder, and his dangling arm fouled the balance of his body and swung grotesquely in the way of the knee he was laboriously hoisting under him. When he got foot to ground, the ground rolled away and brought him down again on his face, sobbing with pain and desperation; but he touched rock with his outflung hand, and groping his way up it inch by inch, got a firm hold, and dragged himself up again to his knees, to his feet. Swaying, lurching, holding frantically by the rock, he struggled round to face the two who did not even know he was there.

He gripped his bleeding shoulder in his right hand, and thrust himself off from the rocks, blundering toward them in a top-heavy run; and then the crushing darkness swirled round him again in strangling folds and brought him down, and for a moment vision and hearing deserted him, and nothing was left but the agonized sensitivity of his fingertips, flayed and quivering from the very touch of the withered grass.

So he never saw Annet draw the muzzle of the gun to her breast and settle it, smiling—though the darkness would have hidden the lovely and terrible quality of the smile—against her heart.

Hearing came back to him with a crash, swollen sounds battering his flinching ears like bomb bursts. Then as suddenly they dwindled and separated, congealing into recognizable order, though for some seconds they made no sense, because he had no strength to turn his head. He thought there was a voice urging something, and that must have been Annet, and another voice that recoiled and refused, in helpless horror, and yet with so little strength or conviction that it was plain it could not long go on refusing. And then a clipped impact, a sharp, faint cry, and something falling.

Two things falling. One of them flew and rolled, ricocheting from the rocks, and at the end of its course along the grass stung his outstretched hand. He closed his fingers on it, and it was hard and heavy, and fitted snugly into his palm. A flung stone. Not just any stone, he knew it by its weight and texture. One of Jane's specimens of galena. One of the boys must have had it in his pocket. It didn't belong on top here, it came from below, by the old lead workings.

One of the boys! That shook him into full consciousness again, and drove him to his knees, heavy head thrust erect by main force, clouded eyes straining. The mated shadows under the Altar had been torn apart, something small and metallic had whined against stone in falling. The gun, struck clean out of Blacklock's hand, lay three yards away in the grass; a pencil beam of light from his little flashlight searched for it frantically and found it. On either side shadows came running, a ring of footsteps circled him like a chain, as he flung himself after the gun and snatched it from the ground.

He was straightening up with it in his hand when another light found him, pinned him, held him transfixed and dazzled. Someone had come scrambling round the slabs of the Altar, running with the rest, and there halted suddenly to launch and steady the beam of a strong torch upon him. For a long moment he crouched blinded in the glare, his head thrown back, his eyes dilated and blank as glass in a contorted face of desperation and anguish, quite motionless.

He could have fired into the light, he could have taken one at least of these encroaching shadows with him out of the world, but he did not. They were all round him, they knew him, there was no escape. He knew it was all over. It stared plain in the tragic mask of his face that he knew, and had accepted his end. He looked full into the light, and suddenly lifted the gun to his own temple and squeezed the trigger.

The shot and Annet's brief, heartrending shriek of grief and loss exclaimed and recoiled together from rock to rock, eddying away into infinite distance. The beam of light quivered in a shaking hand, and drooped after the collapsing body into the grass.

When George Felse reached the spot half a minute later, with Lockyer hard on his heels, when Jane Darrill came forward on unsteady legs, the flashlight dangling in her hand and the two boys silent and shaken beside her, Dominic still clutching a fragment of barites in his hand, Annet was crouched in the trampled grass with her lover's body cradled in her arms, her cheek pressed against his head, the small, powder-rimmed hole in his temple hidden by the fall of her black hair. Body, arms, head, she was folded about him with all her force, as though she would never again unclasp and separate herself from him. She did not move when they came to her, or speak, or show in any way that she was aware of them.

Faintness like a smothering velvet curtain swung between Tom's eyes and the figures that closed in from either side. Snatches of voices reached him. He heard George telling somebody to "see what you can do for Tom," and then there were hands carefully taking hold of him, turning him on his back, detaching his rigid fingers from the tuft of long grass by which he had been trying to drag himself along. Someone raised him a little against a knee. Through

his own personal darkness he was spasmodically
aware of light turned upon him. The hands that were
busy at his blood-soaked shoulder were a man's, but
the light touch that supported his head was surely a
woman's. He opened his eyes and looked up into
Jane's face, softly lit from below, drawn, subdued,
great-eyed with shock.

The pendulum of consciousness reached its stead-
iest, and the light its brightest. He lifted his head
with an effort, craning round Jane's supporting arm.
Someone stood between him and Annet, a young,
tall silhouette, frozen still for awe of death.

"Dom, go down and phone from the box," said
George's voice. "Call the station and tell them it's an
ambulance job, urgent. Then call Superintendent
Duckett, and tell him what's happened. And then go
home. You hear?"

Low-voiced, Dominic said, "Yes," and offered no
arguments. He uncrooked his aching finger from
about the piece of barites he wouldn't, after all, have
to throw, and let it fall dully into the ground; then,
remembering that Jane had wanted it, groped for it
again and returned it to his pocket. He felt beneath
the dangling plummet of specimens for coppers, and
his hand, numbed from long tension, fumbled clum-
sily with pennies it could not feel except as cold-
ness. He dragged his gaze from Annet and went as
he was bidden, walking to the edge of the westward
slope with the abnormal firmness and matter-of-
factness of one still in shock; but once over the edge
he came to himself, and set off running and leaping
down the traverse of grass like a hare.

His going uncovered the two figures clasped in-
dissolubly together in the grass. Annet had not
moved. Withdrawn into herself in the sealed silence

of bereavement, she crouched in the classic shape of mourning. Tom strained to keep his eyes upon her, and his own pain was only an irritation that fretted at his bitter concentration without bringing him ease, a threat that filmed his vision over with faintness when most he desired to continue seeing. He moaned when they eased the coat away from his wound, but he shook the encroaching dark from him, and fastened on Annet still like a famished man.

George had dropped to his knees beside those motionless, fused lovers, and was putting back gently the curtain of black hair that shrouded their faces, to look closely at the wound that had brought them down together. But even when he had satisfied himself, what was there he could have to say to Annet? She knew Peter Blacklock was dead; there was no need for anyone to break that news to her. There was no need for words at all; there was no aspect of this death and this survival she had not already understood. And George had nothing to say. But without fuss, as one doing what was there to be done, he took her chin in his hand and lifted her head erect, gently loosened her fingers from their rigid clasp, and unwound her arms from about her dead. He lifted the limp body out of her embrace and laid it down in the grass, and taking Annet by the hands, drew her to her feet.

And she turned to him, not away from him! She turned to him voluntarily, leaning forward into his shoulder with a broken sigh. He held her for a while, gently and impersonally; and when she raised her head and stood back from him he took away his arms gently and gradually, and let her stand alone.

"Miles!"

He had not said one word or made one movement

until then, only stood motionless and apart in the darkness by the rocks, biding his time. Tom had forgotten him until he heard the measured and muted voice say, "I'm here."

"Take Annet down to my car, and drive her home. She'll go with you now."

CHAPTER 11

$\mathbf{H}$e came up out of a well
shaft of weakness and slight fever, tossed into half
consciousness, aware of faces bending over him, and
of a bright, bare whiteness which was a small room
at the Cottage Hospital, though he did not know that
until later. He said aloud the most urgent thing he
had drawn up with him out of his uneasy dreams, not
realizing how often he had said it before.

"Annet didn't know. She had no part in it. She
knew nothing about murder—or robbery."

The faces showed no surprise. They soothed him
quickly. "It's all right. We know. Nobody blames
Annet."

"She only wanted to go to him to persuade him to
come back with her and give himself up."

"Yes, don't worry. Don't worry about anything. We
know."

"She said—it had no virtue unless he chose it himself. She refused to go away with him. She wanted—"

"Yes, you told us. It's all right, we know everything."

She wanted him to kill her, he had tried to say, but it stuck in his throat and filled him with such a leaden burden of pain that he sank again into the drowning depths of his isolation. None of them had heard what he had heard, or suffered what he had suffered. They could look her in the face again, live within touch and sound and sight of her and find it bearable. But he never could. He didn't even ask after her. It was no use, there was nothing there for him. His only right in her was to proclaim her immaculate; and that he did as often as he drifted back into consciousness, purging his overburdened soul and bleeding his frustrated love out of him in anxious witness to her innocence.

"Don't let them blame Annet. She didn't do anything—"

"No, no, don't worry. Annet will be all right."

Later, when he was convalescent, propped up on pillows with his shoulder swathed, they all came to see him, bringing with them fragments which were not now so much pieces of a puzzle as handfuls of stones to pile on a cairn, marking the place memorable for a disaster or a death. Or maybe an achievement. Or a discovery. Such as his own limitations, or the child's discovery, uncomfortable but salutary, that fire burns, or if you get out of your depth you may drown.

It was George Felse who brought him the few pieces that actually were gaps in the puzzle: the inquisitive small boy who had reported the motorcycle in Mrs. Brookes's backyard, the message the vicar had brought, and the precise reason behind Annet's flight from Fairford.

"The bike seemed to point to Stockwood, who had the loan of one of the estate B.S.A.s for the weekend.

He couldn't have been the first fellow, six months ago, but that didn't let him out altogether, there was no certainty they were the same. And he'd let himself in for suspicion, anyhow, first by lying about his whereabouts, and then by saying he'd spent the time with a woman, but refusing to name the woman."

He said nothing about his own barely tenable theory that the woman might, just might, have been Regina Blacklock; a theory they'd never had to investigate, after all, thank God!

"Moreover, he had a prison record. He did a year for his part in a holdup job, through getting mixed up with some girl, and his wife got a decree nisi against him into the bargain. He was an obvious possibility. But when Mrs. Brookes came up with the item of evidence about Annet's *father,* that let Stockwood out. He wasn't old enough by years. When I spoke to you on the phone I had a kind of idea that *you* knew something you weren't exactly rushing to tell, something that seemed to fit."

"I did," said Tom, remembering that, too, as something infinitely distant and unreal. "I thought I did. But it doesn't matter now. It was wrong, anyhow. So you didn't have to find out who Stockwood's woman was."

"No, we didn't have to, but as it turned out, we did. The Superintendent let his name drift into the handout to the evening paper on Saturday, and she came forward in a hurry, all flags flying, to say he'd been with her. She was his wife, you see. She *is* his wife," he corrected himself with a broad smile. "Talk about good out of evil, the Bloome Street case put paid to that divorce, once and for all. I doubt if he could lose her again even if he tried."

Sidetracked out of the too deeply worn cutting of his own obsessive grief, Tom followed this strange by-product of murder with awakening wonder. "But if it was his wife, why wouldn't he say so?"

"Because it had taken him months to get her even to talk to him again, and he wanted her back, and had just brought her to the point of surrender. It was a triumph that she'd let him work his way in and stay those few days. But he knew he was still on probation, and he was terrified that if he gave it away that he'd lived with her again she'd think he was trying to fix her, force her hand by preventing the divorce from going through. He knew her well enough to know she had a temper, and she was badly hurt the first time. She might very well have turned on him and told him to go to hell if she'd thought he was framing her. But when she heard the police were interested in his movements, she came like a fury to protect him. That's one happy ending, at least, even if we only reached it by accident."

"I'm glad somebody got some good out of it," said Tom.

"So we were left with a motorbike that could be one of the three they keep at Cwm, but didn't have to be, and this idea of the man who could pass for Annet's father. When it turned out that the vicar had brought the message that sent Annet out that night, that seemed to make him a possibility, at first sight. But obviously he spent the whole of Sunday at Comerford—he had Communion and two services, and he always puts in an appearance at Sunday School, too—and in any case there were immediately other inferences to be drawn. The message he brought was from the choir, so he said, but in practice that meant from the choirmaster. Peter Blacklock—well, who had such privileged access to Annet as he did? He could and did ride one of the estate three-fifties up and down to the plantations when it suited him—nobody in his senses would use an E-type Jag for a job like that, where he wanted to be inconspicuous—and he could very well pass for Annet's father. And it was only a startling thought at first sight," said George, looking back at it somberly from the light of knowledge, "and then not for along."

"But he was at church, too. And at choir practice on the Friday night. He rang up afterward and asked why Annet hadn't come—whether she was ill."

"That was part of the campaign. He had to know whether they'd done anything decisive, like going to the police. Annet was sure they wouldn't, but he wasn't happy, he wanted to know. He divided his time very delicately. On Thursday he took Annet to Birmingham. On Friday at dusk he left her there and came back to choir practice, and went through that little performance of enquiring after Annet, offering to go round and see her if she was fit to have visitors. And then he went back to her, and stayed with her until Sunday morning. What happened on Saturday night you know. It wasn't planned, of that I'm certain. It happened out of desperation and chance opportunity. He never intended murder, but he needed money. He needed it badly, and it was there winking at him, and only this old man in the way. He gave Annet the wedding ring, and neither she nor we will ever know exactly why. It may have been just cover for what he'd done. Or it may be the real reason why he went into the shop, to buy the thing for her, the symbol of the permanence of their love and the secret dream marriage that was all they would ever have, and the other thing may have happened on a disastrous impulse, because the time and the circumstances offered, and he was fuller of longing for her than he could bear. I don't know. In some ways I underestimated him; maybe I'd better not even try to guess.

"Well, that was Saturday. And on Sunday he came to morning service in Comerford, to be seen, to be fortified by other people's assumption of his normality until he almost believed himself that everything was normal. He didn't know until he went back that the old man was dead. He'd asked his deputy to play on Sunday evening. That happened sometimes, no one thought anything about it. And he didn't come back until he brought Annet home on Tuesday evening, and parted from her behind the Hallowmount."

"And it was Annet who hid the briefcase?"

"Yes, that was Annet. She hid it in their old place, and walked over the crest and came face to face with you."

With difficulty, his face turned away, Tom asked, "She told you about it?"

"She told us. No reason why she shouldn't now."

"But she didn't know what it was. He can't have told her."

"All she knew was that it was their savings, the only funds they had, and they wanted it ready to hand, because soon—very soon, they were determined on that now—they were going away together for good."

Tom turned from that because it cut too near, and he could not bear to look at it yet. "I should have thought it might have been awkward with the servants. I know there was no reason to go closely into his movements, but if you had, they'd have told you he was absent most of the relevant time."

"What servants?" said George simply, and smiled. "The days of resident staffs are over, even in houses like Cwm. Hadn't you realized? Well, why should

you, come to think of it, it wouldn't be a revolution
that hit you, any more than it did me. Nobody has
servants, these days. You have dailies who come in
to clean, mornings, and maybe one who cooks if
you're lucky, but only during the day, at that, and not
weekends. Weekends Madam does her own cooking
now, and if she's away, her husband eats out. Stockwood had been sent off to his wife, and delighted
with the opportunity, Mrs. Bell had said she had her
daughter and the baby coming over the weekend, so
she couldn't oblige, and Blacklock had said that was
all right, he could manage. Their regular early girl,
who came first thing in the morning to clean, had a
key, and most often she never saw him, anyhow. No,
there was no difficulty there. One appearance at
choir practice and one at church, and everyone had
a normal picture of his weekend, and was convinced
he'd spent it here."

"I suppose," said Tom, staring fixedly at the stiff
hem of the sheet, "it must have been going on for
some time—between him and Annet?"

"That depends what you mean. I think he must
have loved her almost from the moment she began to
work for his wife. Certainly very soon afterward."

Very soon afterward! How could he help it, married to that busy public figure whose capacities for
private warmth he must have exhausted long ago,
and brought into daily contact with that glowing,
ardent, conserved potential of beauty and passion,
whose very extravagance would be like drink to him
in a desert?

"I don't know when he made the fatal mistake of
betraying it. Probably not long before they planned
that first abortive flight together. I think it must
have been a new discovery then. She couldn't, I
think, fail to respond as soon as she knew. And once

she loved him," said George, weighing the words and dropping them onto the cairn one by one, "he was done for. Between the two of them he didn't have much chance."

"*She* didn't make him a murderer," said Tom, taking fire. "I don't see how anyone could blame Annet."

"*I'll* go with you on that. So would most people. Everyone, probably," said George ruefully, "except Annet. *She* knew. When it was too late, she knew what she'd done. If she'd failed to respond he would have made himself content with what he had, glimpses of her, proximity, company, the pleasure of working together, until time and his glands eased up on him, and turned the whole thing into a nice, gentle, father-and-daughter affection. She made the mistake of taking him at his word. It was only a very little step from that to loving him. And once she began, *she* was the dominant. She'd dragged him unwittingly into a situation that wasn't beyond her scope, but was more than he could bear. To her love was for loving, not a passive thing, and once she'd accepted him he couldn't go on fondly dreaming it, he was forced to turn it into action. The first try was a failure, but the second—more cautious this time, just a rehearsal—came off. When they wandered past Worrall's shop that Saturday evening they'd had just two nights together, and the world was on fire. Once he'd tasted that, how could he let it go? They had to get away together, for good this time. Nothing else would do. But for that he had to have money, a fair sum of money, not the twenty pounds or so for petrol and day-to-day spending he kept in his pockets by Regina's grace, but enough to break free and start again somewhere else. And money in that quantity was what he hadn't got—almost the only thing he hadn't got."

"I know," said Tom, low-voiced. "It takes a bit of realizing. The cars, and the clothes—and every-thing."

"He was a pretty good solicitor once in his own right, but when he married her the administration of her estates took up all his time. It never occurred to her that she ought to pay him for it, everything she had was his. He only had to admire something, only to like it, much less want and ask for it, and she'd buy it and give it to him. There wasn't anything she wouldn't give him—except the solid salary his work was worth to her. She wasn't possessive about her money, she just didn't think about it, and it never occurred to her that he could feel cramped and humiliated by having to ask her for what she never grudged. Maybe he didn't miss it himself until he wanted something he couldn't ask her to buy for him. So like any adolescent kid pushed to desperation, he took the twentieth-century short cut—a quick at-tack and a clean sweep of the most expensive-looking cases in the shop. But like any adolescent kid frightened out of his wits by his own first act of violence, he hit too hard, and there was more than a headache and the insurance money to pay for it. No, between those two he didn't have much chance. But Annet had the honesty and the courage to look squarely at her own part in it, and take rather more than her share of blame on her shoulders. She was quite prepared to give her own life away to save him from making bad worse, to try to make some sort of restitution to him and to the world. Regina is and will always be injured and blameless."

"And yet she thought the world of him," said Tom, honestly baffled. "And she *is* a good woman."

"A good woman, but not a good wife. She was kind but not considerate," said George reflectively, "lavish but not generous, intelligent but without imagination."

Chilled by the rounded knell of the falling phrases, Tom said, "It sounds like an epitaph."

"It turned out to be an epitaph," said George, "only not hers."

Miles and Dominic came, brought him fruit and cigarettes and dutiful greetings from their parents, and sat by his bed making somewhat constrained conversation for half an hour. They told him the ordinary things, scraps of news from school and the harmless social calendar of the village. They were punctilious in addressing him as "sir," and retaining, with an effort they hid, on the whole, very well, traces of the schoolboy in their own phraseology. He understood, as once he would not have understood, that this was a delicate device on their part to restore the distance between them that would make life easier for him.

And he played their services back to them neatly, and was grateful, as once he would not have been grateful.

The Becks came, side by side in tacit truce, united by the catastrophe that had overtaken them. Whether Mrs. Beck had lied or told the truth, for all practical purposes Annet belonged to both of them, and for her sake they were compelled to draw together. They explained to him that they planned to give her and themselves a fresh start by moving south to a new home. They had found a small house in a village near Cambridge, which was Mrs. Beck's native district. There'd be a job for Annet there, within easy reach, and new friends, new scenes, a new life would soon set her up again. But of course he must come back to them when he came out of hospital, next week; they would still be at Fairford for several weeks yet, and he would need time to look round and find fresh lodgings.

He breathed the more easily for knowing that they were leaving. But for that he would have had to hand in his resignation and get away to fresh fields himself. It would be impossible to live in daily contact with her now, having witnessed what he had witnessed. There are things that should not be seen.

He asked after her; it was like devouring his own heart. He didn't, after all, need their answers; he could see her plainly enough moving through her sunless days, the shell of Annet, silent, secluded, drained deep in unhappiness, surviving her loss because she must. Life can't just stop. Their version softened the picture, made it more encouraging. They offered him a sad little greeting from her; he did not believe in it, but he could not imagine why they should make it up.

Only after they had left did it occur to him that they regarded him as blessedly safe, as one who would be good for her, as the means of turning their perilous liability into a tamed, respected, domesticated schoolmaster's wife. They wanted him to take her off their hands, and provide her with the halo of a real wedding ring.

Oh, no, he thought, not me. I've drawn back into my depth. I've given up. I know when I'm licked. On Annet's plane of love there are precious few of us can operate with dignity, and, God help me, I'm not one.

And Jane came. Jane came oftenest. She was as offhand as ever, didn't make any great fuss of him, didn't try to tell him he'd done anything heroic when he knew he'd done something stupid and short-sighted, of which he was ashamed. She told him that Regina, shocked beyond words in her respectability, but surely in her heart, too—for there was a heart somewhere under all the crust of offices—had taken up her roots for a while and gone abroad.

"And the Becks have got a cottage somewhere down south—Cambridgeshire, I think. They hope to be in before Christmas."

"I know," he said, "they told me. It's the best thing they could do, for Annet and themselves." He hesitated over what he wanted most to ask, but it came out of itself before he was aware: "Have you seen Annet?"

"Yes," said Jane, giving him one of those slightly disconcerting looks that had once made him speculate on whether she had designs on him, but now only warned him that she was probably making allowances for him.

"She'll live," she said shortly, before he could feel himself forced to ask. And as quickly she looked up again, herself startled by the brusque sound of it. "Not being flippant about it," she said crossly. "I meant it literally. She *will* live—a hundred percent, someday. Well, ninety, say. Which is more than most people manage. She's far too positive and alive ever to have wanted to die, no matter what debts she conceived she owed and was willing to honor. If you think the stuff she has in her can be battered out of shape by this or any other experience, my boy, you can think again. Don't worry about Annet. And don't feel sorry for her. But don't kid yourself, either," she added honestly, "that you'll ever get her, because I don't think you will. Sorry, but there it is."

He didn't say that he agreed with her, or that he

had already withdrawn from the field and acknowledged defeat. He didn't say that he was just becoming reconciled to the idea of setting his sights,
someday, on a less impossible target. There was
only one Annet, now and forever out of reach; but in
his new humility he was prepared to listen respectfully to the small, dry voice deep within him, assur-
ing him that he could think himself damned lucky if
someday he was able to settle for someone like Jane.

When he came out of hospital and returned to
Fairford it was already November. The Hallowmount withdrew itself at morning and evening into
mist, shrouding the Altar and its ring of decrepit
trees. He wondered if the small, unaccountable
ground wind had abandoned, until next spring, its
nightly ascent by the old paths to the old places,
where Annet had vanished for a while into her secret
world, and whether the reverberations of her tragedy had already seeped away like spilled blood into
that already saturated soil.

He had found new lodgings in Comerford, and he
began to assemble his belongings in preparation for
the move. He was in the hall one evening, digging
out his windjacket and climbing boots from the
cupboard, when the knocker rapped gently to an-
nounce a visitor.

Tom dropped his boots and went to open the door.
Miles Mallindine looked at him across the thresh-
old, composed, dogged, dignified, with a handful of
late roses. In the sheltered garden close to the river
they bloomed until Christmas unless discouraged.

Not everyone knows when he's beaten. Not everyone can recognize when he's out of his class. There
was—wasn't there?—an obligation. In pure kindness
someone ought to warn him.

"May I come in? Mrs. Beck said I could drop round tonight."

He was in already. He had a very unobtrusive way of moving, that took him where he wanted to go, even against opposition, without actually looking aggressive or even noticeably determined. And he held the roses as one neither embarrassed nor ashamed at displaying his intentions. He wasn't smiling; sieges like the one he was contemplating are no joke.

"Oh, of course! Annet's in the study, doing some typing for her father, I think." Never had she been so gentle with his pretensions, or so willingly segregated herself behind the clacking of the keys, over his interminable notes.

He let Miles go halfway across the hall, and then he couldn't let him go the rest; not without a word of caution, at least, because he was heading gallantly in full armor for a sickening fall.

"Miles—"

Miles halted and turned, surprised and wary, brown eyes wide. The curled lashes arched toward his brows. Faint color came and went in his thin, shapely cheeks. He looked like his mother; Eve disarmingly young and apparently vulnerable, but already, beyond mistake, a dangerous person.

"Miles, I shouldn't. There's nothing there now for you. The best's gone."

"I know," said Miles, not retreating a step.

He was doing this badly, but he couldn't stop now. The detachment they had so considerately restored to him he was endangering again, but at least this was between himself and Miles, man to man again with no witnesses.

"She won't want to look at any man, not for a long

time yet. And even if she ever does, what she's got
left to give—"

"I know," said Miles, honestly, ruefully, even gratefully, but without the slightest intimation that it
made any difference.

It was something in the voice that made Tom
pause. He caught the maturing intonations of patience and forbearance, and turned with the sudden
shock of recognition to confront himself. Here we go
again, he thought. You were going to save Annet,
weren't you? You, without a clue to what went on
inside of her, or what she was capable of! Now
you're setting out to save Miles, and just about as
likely to find him in need of it, and just about as well
equipped to make a hash of it. How do you know
what he has it in him to do? Just because you've
bitten off more than you can chew, and been forced
to own it, does *he* have to give up, too? Wake up and
stand by for a shock: you *can* be outdone!

He drew back into silence, carefully, respectfully,
and looked at the whole setup again. But what future
was there in it? Next week Annet was going with her
parents to Cambridgeshire, and if there was one
thing certain it was that they'd never come back to
Comerford.

Well, next year Miles was going to Queens', wasn't
he? Not that the issue depended on such small,
convenient accidents as that, he thought, studying
the boy's courteous, wary company face. There was
nothing here now for Tom Kenyon, no. But might
there not be something for Miles Mallindine? Someday, if his patience held out?

For Miles there'd have to be. Because he had no
intention of ever giving up. He knew what he wanted,
he meant to have it. The whole, or half, or whatever

there was to be won at last. He was never going to settle for any substitute.

And Annet, whole or broken, sick or convalescent, had her values right. Sooner or later she'd recognize what it was she was being offered.

"All right, forget it," said Tom. "You go ahead your own way. And good luck!"

Miles said, "Thank you!" and for a moment it was touch-and-go whether he would add, "—*sir!*" It was on the tip of his tongue, but he snatched it back generously, flashing for one brief instant the engaging and impudent smile he had inherited from Eve. Then he turned, patient, stubborn and profoundly sure of himself, and went to Annet with his roses.